SAVING LIVES IS MEANT TO BE ABOVE POLITICS. In a troubled health system, where patient outcomes and personal gain are intertwined, Harvey Pearce discovers a disturbing and dangerous truth.

In *The Cut*, Dr Harvey Pearce is an emergency specialist who has spent a career looking after the sickest patients and improving emergency care. When he uncovers politically orchestrated activities that kill patients, harm staff, hide deficiencies and hinder progress, he becomes determined to find a solution.

Across the city, episodes of patient injury and preventable deaths continue despite Harvey's struggles with bureaucracy. He drives to investigate these events, and their sinister connections, whilst the establishment resists his efforts and its leaders continue to tolerate catastrophes.

Harvey finds a grounding for his efforts through his podcasts. They fuel his aspirations as he struggles to put things right. The podcasts propose a pragmatic approach, offering a view that life could be better navigated with a closer focus on what really matters.

But Harvey is quickly confronted with desperate and ruthless players who turn his efforts at reform into a perilous game with critical stakes.

MARCUS KENNEDY is a retired emergency physician, who, like Harvey, spent many years working in different parts of emergency and public health services. As a clinician, researcher, leader and administrator, he wrote many things, but nothing like this. *The Cut* is his first novel.

THE **CUT**

MARCUS KENNEDY

AREX
PRESS

Published by AREX Press
Albert Park, Victoria, 3206, Australia

First published in 2020

Copyright © Marcus Kennedy 2020
https://marcuskennedy.net/
The moral rights of the author have been asserted.

All rights reserved. Except as permitted under the Australian Copyright Act 1968 (for example, a fair dealing for the purposes of study, research, criticism or review), no part of this book may be reproduced, stored in a retrieval system, communicated or transmitted in any form or by any means without prior written permission. All inquiries should be made to the author.

 A catalogue record for this book is available from the National Library of Australia

Title: The Cut
Author: Kennedy, Marcus (1958 –)
Paperback 978-1-922337-73-3
E Book 978-1-922337-52-8

Cover design by Leah Morgan. – leah.morgan.design@gmail.com
Editing by Ann Bolch from A Story to Tell – www.astorytotell.com.au
Design and Production by Green Hill. – info@greenhillpublishing.com
Typeset Adobe Garamond Pro 11/16

Disclaimer

The material in this publication is of the nature of general comment only and does not represent professional advice. It is not intended to provide specific guidance for particular circumstances, and it should not be relied on as the basis for any decision to take action or not take action on any matter, which it covers.

FOR LORNA, who graciously tolerated the writing of this and lived through all the moments that led up to it!

AND A WORD OF THANKS to the many people (patients, colleagues and friends) who provided me with a trove of experiences and stories during my 35 years-plus in public health. Some of the challenges of that rewarding world are included here.

THANKS ALSO to CE for an early read of the manuscript and encouragement, to JK and the anonymous manuscript reviewer at Writers Victoria for insightful, inspiring and constructive advice. I'm grateful to all the friends and family whose ears have been bent as I tried to find my way through the process of writing this novel!

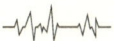

THIS IS A WORK OF FICTION

Names, characters, organisations, events, clinical scenarios and incidents are all the products of the author's imagination or are used fictitiously. Any perceived resemblance in this story to actual persons, living or dead, or actual events is purely coincidental.

The podcasts contained have not been broadcast or published as podcasts and are the thoughts of the author, and also draw on fictional examples and content.

A WARNING

I ask: when the truth's not truth and we all lie,
What are we then but insects in a web?
The crawler came and smote with poison sly,
Despite our cries and curses we lay dead
Turned paranoid by watching our own backs
Our lack of prudent questions left us blind
There was no warning for the beast's attack
In short order it defeated human kind
It was no terrorist no psychopath
That caused humanity's untimely end
'Twas fear that caused the chilling aftermath
No longer could we find a needed friend
So if you value good – feel it's a must
Be brave, go foster honesty and trust.

—AVK

Glossary

Because this story wanders into the medical world, I have included some terms to explain some of the less known references and acronyms:

AMI: Acute myocardial infarction; heart attack.

AUSMAT: Australian Medical Assistance Teams (AUSMAT) – multi-disciplinary health teams responding to international incidents.

ASIO: The Australian Security Intelligence Organisation is Australia's national security agency responsible for protection from espionage, sabotage, acts of foreign interference, politically motivated violence, attacks on the Australian defence system and terrorism.

Cath Lab: Cardiac Catheter Lab where heart attack patients are treated using angiographic and stent techniques.

ED: Emergency Department. (Previously 'Casualty' or 'Accident and Emergency'.)

EMS: Emergency Medical Service – Ambulance service providing pre-hospital care by paramedics.

ER: American ED; Medical TV drama, NBC, from 1994.

Ketamine: Intravenous anaesthetic and hallucinogenic agent (human and animal uses) and drug of abuse.

Mastenyl: A fictitious synthetic narcotic.

Propofol: Intravenous anaesthetic agent in common use.

RCA: Root Cause Analysis – Modern health systems process for systematic investigation of the causes and issues underlying an incident or major error. Standardised investigation method applied in all health jurisdictions and often monitored by government.

RTA: Road Traffic Accident.

The House of God: A satirical medical novel by Samuel Shem (pen name for psychiatrist Dr Stephen Bergman) first published 1978. A medical equivalent of Heller's *Catch 22*.

Chapter 1

Saturday March 16, 2019

There's something special about that smell – the Saturday night in the Emergency Department special blend. Stale alcohol and blood, rough-living bodies last washed at best a week ago, vodka and vomit thanks to an experimenting teenager. Faeces and urine leaked with unbearable embarrassment from someone who deserves privacy and dignity. Then the futile chemicals intended to clean and hide it all.

Gloves, white overalls, waterproof boots – the cleaner finishes and no one would know there had been a pool of blood and vomit in the corner a minute ago.

'Forty-two in the waiting room at the start of the shift. What chance do we have to catch up with that?' grumbles a millennial nurse on her second shift in the ED.

'Mummy it hurts a lot.' Four-year-old girls don't deserve pain.

'Don't worry lovely they'll be here to look after you soon.' Mothers don't deserve to see their children waiting in pain.

All Jess Goldman can think about is getting ten minutes to have some dinner. Maybe another five for a coffee.

Triage announces: 'Incoming, three ambulances from a car crash. Police car versus stolen SUV. Seven minutes. One stable femur fracture, one chest, one intubated head injury with no blood pressure. Trauma team activated and code paged. Surgeon is responding.'

The police arrive at the back entrance. One either side of a dapper gent with a debonair moustache, three-piece suit, and briefcase. Who has a briefcase these days?

The intern picks up another crooked arm from the waiting pile and reflects, 'I hope that guy I sent home with the headache is OK.'

The intercom interrupts with more volume than is really necessary. 'Paging Dr Goldman to Resusc. Urgent page Dr Goldman.'

Goldman breathes out. Dinner can wait, just like lunch did.

An executive-looking chap with fear all over his face has chest pain and needs to get to a stent ten minutes ago. His ECG looks like a line of tombstones.

Three nurses are scrubbed and waiting in resusc for the traumas, another ready to scribe, medical-student runners lined up. IV's primed, blood ordered, radiographer on the way.

'Harvey, we may need you in resusc.' Goldman calls out.

'No problem, I'll finish the five things I'm doing in a flash.' The professor smiles kindly at the pale panting old man whose wide eyes and cold hands say it all.

How does he never seem rattled?

Raucous ambulance sirens, one maybe two. I don't know why they need the sirens on in the car park. We know they're coming, there's no traffic. The paramedics park their horses, discard their spurs and wheel in the three from the RTA. Three wise monkeys coming through the door. Emergency Medical Services and police everywhere.

The first patient crashes on arrival, whiter than the sheet, drip tissued, tube down too far, and the EMS dude says, 'He was fine a minute ago'.

'Thanks Professor Pearce,' says the old man's daughter, 'you've been so kind. We'll be here when you get back…'

They'd been there ten hours already. Not going anywhere soon. No beds - again.

By tonight we'll have a dozen in the corridors.

'Mummy it's getting worse and no one is coming.'

And in the waiting room toilet Alfredo Bipolar preens his stash, adjusts his waistcoat, and launches into top voice with accompanying stagecraft:

'Libiam ne' lieti calici
Che la bellezza infiora,
E la fuggevol ora
S'inebri a voluttà.
Libiam ne' dolci fremiti
Che suscita l'amore…'

I guess Traviata is better than a sermon from Jesus Christ or a lesson from a Martin Luther King reincarnation like last week. Everyone hates shifts at triage.

Dead. Jess called it on the first trauma. No chance of winning there. They all shift their attention to the young woman with the head injury. The driver is the one with the fractured femur. Her pipe and paraphernalia are still hanging out of her jeans pocket.

'What do you need me to do?' asks Harvey.

'Don't worry about these,' says Jess – 'check the diabetic next door, will you, and see if those residents in Pod 2 need a hand. They're week two and drowning in it.'

―⋀⋀⋀―

The adjacent cubicle is frantic with activity. Harvey parts the curtains and stands quietly at the end of the bed, surveying the scenario. It's a technique and a discipline that emerged after his first decade or so in the business. No matter the level of chaos or the urgency of a patient's problem, there is always time — always has to be time — to look and listen and see and hear what was happening. From that comes the 'what to do next'. It never took long. In a matter of a minute, and sometimes seconds, he could see the picture emerge from the whirling activity.

In this room he saw a teenage girl on the trolley, maybe eighteen or nineteen. Sweaty, breathing rapidly, pink lips but a white ring around them, which was paler than the rest of her very pale skin. She coughed. Eyes wide, worried. No, frightened. IV lines in both arms, fluids running on one side, staff connecting an infusion pump on the other side. To his right in the corner were a mother and father. They stood silently and worried beside the nurse's desk on which sat a pile of papers, a letter and a small diabetic kit bag open to reveal insulin injections and a glucometer for testing blood sugar.

So, thought Harvey, quite likely she was a newly diagnosed diabetic, still unstable, still learning about her disease, possibly less than one hundred per cent compliant with her treatment (as eighteen-year-olds are prone to be), possibly with an intercurrent chest infection, and parents who hadn't yet come to grips with the impact of a serious chronic disease on the life of their otherwise perfect and beautiful daughter.

The registrar was a recent starter in the ED and Harvey hadn't worked with her. He scanned the name badge — Amy Wong, Emergency Registrar. Amy looked about the same age as the patient and nearly as frightened, so Harvey stood beside her — an action which perceptively slowed her pace, extracting her from her complete immersion in the clinical setting, and required her to focus on this senior colleague, who was now in her space. Over the next couple of minutes Amy confirmed Harvey's end-of-the-bed guesswork. She was on the right track although a bit flustered, so he left her to it, turning back as he moved towards the parents saying, 'Amy, good job. I'd slow the fluids a little and hold off on the insulin infusion till we recheck bloods in half an hour. Some antibiotics for that chest infection would be good, and pop an oxygen mask on – OK?'

All under control.

'Mr and Mrs McDougall?' He'd spotted the name on the chart. A nod confirmed their status as worried parents. 'My name is Harvey Pearce – I'm one of the supervising consultants in the ED today. I will be looking in on Sally today and helping look after her, but at this stage, Dr Wong has everything under control and we're on the right track. Sally is going to be fine but will take the next day or two to settle down and restabilise her diabetes. She'll be home by mid-week.'

Harvey saw the impact of those few words right there on the faces of Sally's parents. Muscles that were taught relaxed a little, eyes that were wide now narrowed and the shoulders that were tense now eased to allow the couple to stand closer. Their two hands met and interlocked. Magic, Harvey thought. I do enjoy that part nearly as much as nailing the diagnosis.

They talk for a few minutes and Harvey shows them to the relatives' room; somewhere they could escape to if needed. The fear these parents have is different to the fear they would have for themselves or each other. More intense, more visceral, uncontainable.

―⋀⋀⋀⋀―

Harvey wanders off to Pod 2 and, for no particular reason, starts humming a vaguely remembered aria.

'Don't ya love Verdi,' calls the drunk on the bench near the door with all the staccato impact of a classic De Niro line. Then he spouts, 'Let's drink from the goblets of joy adorned with beauty, and the fleeting hour shall be adorned with pleasure. Let's drink to the secret raptures of the life I used to have… or something like that.'

He recited the libretto and dropped back to sleep.

Harvey scratches his head and moves on, thinking, 'He probably had a reasonable brain ten years ago. I need to get out of here, I have a plane to catch in the morning. Some sleep would be good.'

Three teenage-looking doctors sit at the desk, each on the phone trying to sell a patient to someone upstairs. Trying to con the bed manager into opening another bed. Trying to bluff the ward nurse with a threat to escalate to admin. Trying to call in a favour from an old mate now doing geriatrics. Trying to remember if there was a rule in '*The House of God*' that would solve this problem?

'Go on James, you owe me, do me a favour and come down and admit this one. I've got another five on the go and haven't had time to take a leak.'

Pain. Pain. Pain.

'Mummy, please.' Too tired to cry now, so just whimper a little. Why is mummy crying too?

The old man's wide eyes relax. Departed. A painless freedom. No time to hold a cold old hand and ease the pathway, or to spend much time with a daughter who now has to say a last cheerio. But she half smiles through tears anyway and seems to understand. Maybe she's been somewhere like this before. Maybe she knows what I would like to be able to do, what I would do, if I had time. He didn't suffer but it's not a nice place to die.

'Clear,' is the call from Ben, the team leader in Resusc Five, and two hundred joules jolt through the chest of a sixty-something, recently retired. Will he get to enjoy his retirement, or will his wife get the life insurance? He wakes up nearly as fast as he passed out and his monitor has changed from fibrillation scribble via flat-line to something looking like a sick heart.

'What the... who kicked me?' he asks with a dumb-struck look on his face. Winner.

The nurse and the consultant smile. That's a good one. The medical student stands with her mouth open, no doubt thinking how remarkably similar the whole experience is to an episode of *'ER'*.

The psych registrar has arrived and says he's looking for a tenor who stopped his meds and is back here courtesy of the police and a neighbour who couldn't tolerate all-night opera.

The middle-aged mum with melanoma is polite. 'Thank you, Alison, you're the best nurse I have ever had looking after me. I know it's hard for you guys here and if I had a choice, I wouldn't come to the ED. You know what I mean. You gave me all the time you could, and you explained, and you were gentle. So, thanks.'

Alison smiles and walks away, groaning inside. 'It's just so noisy, that's the real problem. If the noise would stop, then I could think, the patients could sleep, the rush would slow. I don't know how anyone could work in this forever... How do you do it Professor Pearce?'

'Don't be such a defeatist,' says Harvey. 'Just think of the buzz you get, the lives you save, the difference you can make for someone in their most vulnerable, fear-ridden moment. What could be better?' he says with a wry grin.

She thinks he's being sarcastic. No, his eyes say he's serious.

Alison thinks to herself that crying in the toilet cubicle is pathological, but she can't help herself and just hopes no one hears.

The waiting is over for the four-year old and her mum, and the injection works quickly. Her x-ray is fast-tracked and almost before she knows what's happened, a young orthopaedic registrar called Sarah explains about broken bones and straightening them up and plaster and short sleeps. And then she's awake again. Sarah smiles and mum stops crying, and her arm feels OK. And Sarah draws a big red love heart on the plaster and writes 'from Sarah to a brave girl'.

―⋀⋀⋁⋀⋀―

But how can you deal with all this? It's so frazzled, so full of queues and waiting and risk and systems that don't work and staff that are too junior or too tired. People who care about the patients, but don't know what to do to make it better. Others who don't care and just worry about themselves - their next job or what the boss will yell at them or what the health department bureaucrats will say through their prissy we-really-do-care empathic expressions. It's not surprising that things go wrong.

You know, most people get better; they heal. Recovery is what we expect when we are sick, and it is what the human body does. We're here to help the process along and to turn things in the right direction. The real issue is that all of us know we could do a lot better. All this could be smoother, safer, simpler… more satisfying.

Nowhere and nothing is perfect, and it doesn't matter whether you love it or hate it; it's your obligation to do what you can to make it better.

―⋀⋀⋁⋀⋀―

Someone sitting in a wheelchair, head slumped forward, snores in agreement.

Chapter 2

Brussels

People need to talk, and people need to listen. In 2019 Harvey gave the world something to listen to.

For thirty-eight years, critical care doctors had been gathering in Brussels every March in the not-quite-thawed tail end of the Belgian winter. This year, terrorist activity in Brussels and Paris and on the train between made the cold city colder. Dark-uniformed police and military with their grey weapons littered the town and fuelled a mood of uncertainty and apprehension. Despite this, there were more than five thousand people registered to attend the conference – it was huge. And not because doctors from around the world liked the idea of a junket in Brussels – because really, Brussels in March is a hole, with inevitable rain, incessant wind and barely a glimpse of pathetic sunlight each day. The symposium was, as usual, brilliantly planned and had brought together some of the best and brightest speakers to showcase research, ideas and knowledge from around the world.

Harvey Pearce was a new star in this constellation. He stood at the edge of the stage in the auditorium. The Bozar was the largest theatre at The Square Convention Centre with seating for over two thousand. Harvey peered out through spotlights at the many faces all waiting to hear his words. It was 19 March 2019. The Vincent address at the opening session of the thirty-ninth International Symposium on Critical Care and Emergency Medicine.

Were they ready for what he was about to say?

―⋏⋏⃒⋏⋏―

He had just come from Hotel Le Dixseptiemme, where he'd stayed as part of an annual ritual for each of the last five years. Just a short walk down from The Square towards the centre of the old town, it was a charming hotel – quaint, historic and friendly, oozing the style you'd expect from a grand old building that three centuries before was the residence of a Spanish ambassador. It sat in the centre of the town, among buildings of great beauty and classical architecture, incongruously surrounded by a neighbourhood of shops selling waffles, chocolates, frites and all manner of tat. From the front door, wafts of fried food mixed with a chocolate-flavoured breeze blended with a glimpse of the central station and conference centre up the hill to the right. To the left was a square lined by the tourist traps – victims standing around eating cones of frites and mayonnaise at the wrong time of day.

Harvey had been an emergency physician at Queens Hospital for ten years and in 2012 had come to Brussels for the first time. Freshly appointed to his position as full professor at Sydney University, he was keen to present his findings and research to the largest audience of critical care professionals that gathered annually in one place. His move to work at Queens had been smart, providing him with access to some of the best research supports and a fascinating range of clinical case types and trauma to help him grow as a practitioner, researcher, teacher and manager.

The hospital was the biggest in the metropolitan area, occupying a large part of the Domain area above the harbour and nestling into the large park area bordered by Albert Road and Kings Way. It had two helipads to receive critical trauma, cardiac and intensive care patients from across the state and probably had the best designed ED in the country. Of the almost hundred thousand patients attending each year, many needed critical care and intensive care unit admission.

Harvey had settled into Queens quickly and formed a close bond with Alex Bonito, his head of department and sometime mentor. He'd also settled into Sydney having bought and renovated a small house on the hill in the Domain, capturing some prime real estate with views across the botanical gardens and to the northwest across downtown Sydney. His last home had been an apartment in London for almost eight years. He'd enjoyed the move to a place of his own. No neighbours above or below; quiet families to either side. His place had the potential to be a family home but had remained a rather clichéd residence of a single man of a certain age and style. The kind of man who enjoys books and music and his own company, a comfortable chair with a view of a terrace and a garden that knows just what autumn is meant to look like.

At fifty-three, he wasn't a bad specimen. He'd stayed in shape and still carried some of the strength he'd acquired growing up on the farm. He walked tall and moved purposefully. Harvey engaged the world and kept his eyes up, with the confidence of someone who correctly believes that he is usually right, though not infallible, and with the expression and connection of someone who knows what it means to see and listen to others.

In his view he'd had a reasonable life so far, and was happy enough with his lot, having worked hard forever. His background had provided him with a set of down-to-earth values, little religion, a romantic or nostalgic tendency and no family money to make life that little bit sweeter. A good boarding school afforded Harvey a fine education and he survived without abuse from the priests and brothers. He worked all his university breaks to pay for his medical school and rent. The farm and family support had disappeared when his parents died in a car crash, and their debts ate the remaining cash.

Soon after that, Harvey decided to become an emergency physician – perhaps a reactive decision. It was driven at least in part by his conviction that his parents may not have died if they had been looked after by better skilled paramedics, transferred to the right hospital by an emergency medical helicopter and been cared for in a system that was excellent, safe and reliable – not one that was obviously primitive, under-funded and inconsistent.

There were other reasons to want to spend a working lifetime in the ED. It wasn't all about him and his psycho-baggage. Harvey loved it as a front-line job, raw and challenging, where he could make a difference to people at their sickest and most helpless time. As a bonus, the ED is about as non-routine and stimulating as medicine gets.

For the first ten years or so there was what seemed to be endless learning. Studying for the qualification was one part of the story and yes, that was the first half of the decade, but then there was another five years of growing as a practitioner. About learning the nuances of clinical scenarios, about starting to develop the sense of 'smell' for clinical mischief – the extra nous that turns a young doctor into someone who simply fathoms the depth of an illness or clinical presentation. The someone you want looking after you or your family. Becoming somebody with instinct and intuition as well as knowledge; somebody with a capability for the art of medicine as well as the science. Harvey had the right brain for this and moved quickly in the system. His reputation was unwavering. He was the guy you wanted working on your shift. No matter what mayhem, how big the trauma, how weird the overdose, how 'off' the metabolic presentation, he could get things to flow and the madness to work as well as anyone could expect – on any day, for any shift, for any patient...

Yet he was not a typical super-doc. There were plenty of those underpants-on-the-outside, chest-puffers in the business, because, frankly, the ED attracted them. No, Harvey was a notch back down the scale, didn't need a costume, but probably did have super powers, starting with intuition and sensitivity.

People like that don't stay still and predictably he didn't. Leadership opportunities appeared and his curious mind sought out questions, which had not been answered. He had the right mentors, did the right courses and published research that showed not just a scientific mind but one that understood systems and how they worked – and, more importantly, why they didn't and how to fix them. Harvey maintained that the bulk of health care is just systems for widgets. It's just that the widgets are patients. Certainly, more important and individual and feeling than most other products, but widgets just the same.

He started at Queens at forty-two years of age, Deputy Director and head of ED Quality and Safety systems, and from that time had put more than he needed to into his job. He loved it, enjoyed the challenges, the jousting with bureaucracy to make the impossible happen, the coming and going of trainees, students, staff. He got to influence, to make things happen, to make things better where he could and to see the impact on patients who came through the hospital. He knew they usually didn't have a clue who he was, why the system worked the way it did or what he had done, and it didn't matter. He knew, and he was happy about it. Mostly.

The only problem was that nothing really stayed fixed forever. The strategies of this year seemed to work for a while and the system would run smoothly for a while. Patients moved through, didn't have to wait too long, mistakes and errors happened but were manageable, a few patients or their families said thank you, and complaints were not extraordinary. Then the money would tighten, a management policy would change, the health department would shift the goal posts, attendances would creep up, access hospital beds would decrease as elective surgical targets became flavour of the month. Something always happened to keep the pressure there, and to drive imperfection.

Harvey was weary despite his front-of-the-plane flight yesterday. He had arrived at the hotel late in the afternoon after a delay at Doha, which worked out in his favour by way of a room upgrade. The room was on the third floor of the new wing – it was a mere one hundred and fifty years old. It was larger than the standard rooms and looked over the internal courtyard and its fountain and plants. The décor was familiar; much the same as the room he'd stayed in last year, though there was more space and a pleasant note beside the fruit bowl awaiting him. A returned guest, a regular, comfort in familiarity, all good things. He wanted to keep moving though, get some fresh air and shake out the brain-haze that always came with a long flight. He dropped off his luggage and headed out, walking past the Royal Palace and through the beautifully ordered Park de Bruxelles, retreating to the hotel just as the cold autumn evening arrived.

It was time for a last read through his presentation then an early dinner bought virtuously from the health-food place just down the street. Some drug-induced slumber would follow to counter the jet lag.

Despite this, by 4.30am, Harvey was wide awake. He found the warmest pair of socks he had, pulled on the towelling dressing gown hanging in the robe and sat at the small desk wondering why old hotels were never quite warm enough, and why someone hadn't worked out a better way to endure long distance flights and time zone changes.

The last two weeks at work had been difficult. Harvey half-expected to find more grief as he logged into his email account. It really wasn't a wonderful time to be away at a conference, but he'd made the bookings ages ago and was committed to the talks he was giving over the next three days.

Alex had been off work for ten days after a small heart attack. For a doctor, he was a bad patient: overweight, under-exercised, diabetic, but he was smart and caring and had been both boss and proxy father for Harvey over the last ten years. Harvey worried about him. When Alex had told Harvey about his AMI, the idea of having a 'small heart attack' struck him to be about as sensible a concept as a 'touch of pregnancy' or a 'minor cancer'.

On top of that, a running feud with the local paramedic EMS was coming to a head. A series of their cases reviewed in the last two months, revealed circumstances where patients had presented with poorly managed pain. There was also a collection of not-quite-right clinical outcomes and complications with procedures. The worst of these were two cases where the patients had died shortly after arrival at the ED from potentially manageable conditions, having had lengthy delays and dubious management by the EMS at the roadside.

If that weren't enough another ED physician at Queens had just given notice. Jess Goldman was a good friend and a great doctor, but was burnt-out and had pulled the pin, planning to finish up at Queens in late April. Harvey knew that most emergency physicians teetered on the edge of burnout for much of their careers, once the excitement of the first ten to fifteen years wears off. Many developed quite reasonable strategies for sticking with it, but some didn't, and Jess was one of these, now heading off for therapy, a holiday and a re-evaluation of life's priorities. Hopefully she would find a way back. But slogging away in the ED for five shifts a week could be a trial.

Among the ninety-seven almost certainly irrelevant time-wasting items accumulated in just the last two days in his in-box, he spotted an email from Alex and opened it:

```
From: Alex Bonito <Alexander_Bonito@QH.org>
Subject: Brussels / break a leg
Date: 18 March 2019 at 12:51:19 PM AEST
To: Harvey Pearce
```

Hey Harvey

How goes it? I'm assuming the trip over was reasonable and that you managed to suffer your way through another BC flight/flat bed/wining & dining at altitude etc.

I'm feeling good – quite normal, despite the fun and games of last week, and think I'll be back at work Monday. Yep, the shakeup part (welcome to your mortality) of this is still a bit raw, and yes, I know some work and life changes will need to happen, but so far things have been uncomplicated. Having the stent inserted was straight forward, and our friends in cardiology have been fantastic…I do think I got celebrity level care…but hey, there must be some perks attached to the job!

I just wanted to touch base re your talk. I know I've been a bit preoccupied lately and I didn't really come to grips with the review draft you sent me last week until I sat down this morning to tidy the desk.

Harvey – I read the talk twice and I'm still digesting it. The Vincent address has been a launch pad for great ideas in the past and has seen some challenging ideas presented.

The thing is, I think your material goes somewhere new and offers a map that I wish I'd come across two decades ago! I'm not just stroking your ego either – I like the ideas and want to talk over some of it when you get back.

All the best, break a leg etc.

See you in a week or so.

Cheers

Alex

Harvey sat there just thinking for the next hour, flipping between awareness of his cold feet, the notes on the printed sheets he'd brought with him and the single slide on his computer screen. Harvey had given probably fifty presentations in the last twelve months at various academic meetings, management forums, clinical conferences, and never had he gone in with less than a dozen slides to speak to. Two or three years ago he had abandoned the colour, transitions, animations, and bizarre effects that plague presentation software and taken refuge in minimalist white-on-black slides, making a pact with himself never to use more than fifteen words on a slide! All the same, he'd never gone into a talk with just a single slide and a handful of words. Right now he wondered whether his audience would think this pretentious.

He'd spoken on confronting topics before and liked to challenge an audience or his peers to think differently about a clinical problem or about management of a health-system dilemma. In a way they expected it of him now and he was respected as someone with big and innovative ideas. Sometimes his talks were a bit obtuse and on occasion he had taken his audience on a tangled journey of ideas, arriving in a thought bubble of logic that made them wonder where they were – surrounded by a new perspective.

He struggled with the idea that what he was to talk about today was beyond his remit. Is it all too high-brow, too philosophical, too preachy - for this audience of type A critical-care doctors and nurses? Harvey had been around this circle a dozen times in his mind, in his solitude, in his discipline to challenge himself and his conclusions, and again he ended up in the same place. He didn't know if he was right, but he knew this was what he believed and what he wanted to say.

He wasn't quite sure why he wanted to do this now – perhaps a few sessions with a therapist would answer that for him. His current theory was that his emotional hard-disk was nearing full, so sharing some of the content was a way to offload a series of conclusions that otherwise just sat on his shoulders. Who knows? He also thought that his ideas might be useful to others or at least worth thinking about.

He showered, dressed and went down to the formal dining room, which he guessed would have been a reception room for diplomatic visitors in the past.

The room was richly decorated, but reserved, as were the silent individuals on tables for two – checking phones or browsing local newspapers to avoid connection with another. The perverse corner of his brain wanted to ask the starched woman on the next table if there was anything interesting on her phone…or was she just pretending to read something so she could hide from the other humans in the room?

His breakfast was orange juice, two slices of toast with smoked salmon, and a black coffee. Always the same. Harvey finished then walked out of Le Dixseptiemme and turned up the hill, across cobbled streets and through unpleasant drizzle. By the time he reached the conference centre he felt cold but sharp. Ready.

Chapter 3

Harvey's Colloquium

The conference coordinator began: Ladies and Gentlemen, I am about to welcome to the stage Professor Harvey Pearce; however; let me start by just reflecting briefly on this presentation, the Vincent address. This lecture is delivered each year in the opening session of our symposium and is named for Dr Pierre Vincent, the founder and driving force of this, the most significant scientific meeting of its type in the world. Dr Vincent sought to provide a platform for the presentation of new and challenging critical-care knowledge in this meeting, and in recognising this, each year we honour a leading member of our community by inviting them to present a colloquium that takes us beyond the everyday, drawing the connections between our professional world and the larger world, always with a view to the future.

This year, more than two thousand attendees in this auditorium will see this presentation, whilst an audience of almost the same number will see it relayed live to satellite rooms at this conference venue. We expect a further three thousand critical-care doctors and nurses to see this session streamed live via the internet. For the first time, the Vincent address will also be posted on YouTube for free access by the public.

I would like to introduce Dr Harvey Pearce. Harvey is well known to you as a respected contributor to this symposium over many years. He has published widely in the scientific press with over one hundred and twenty peer-reviewed papers and ten book chapters. He has edited or authored four textbooks. Harvey has also published and delivered many papers in health management, covering topics from process improvement and productivity to realising human potential in the workforce. In recent years, aspects of Harvey's work and writing have attracted attention in the non-healthcare management and governance area and generated interest in the lay press. Please welcome Professor Harvey Pearce.

The applause settled politely while Harvey stood and moved to the lectern, willing the butterflies to depart from his gut and praying that his voice would not emerge thin and tremulous from his dry mouth. Although he knew it wouldn't, he also knew that anxiety is a strange thing and can inject thoughts that make little sense. He looked out into the auditorium, searching for a familiar face or perhaps just any face to focus on. He pressed the button to bring up his single slide.

Thank you so much for such a warm welcome. I greatly appreciate the opportunity to present this address and I am also daunted by the task. In the briefing I received from the organising committee, I was indeed asked to prepare 'a colloquium that draws on your past career, work and research and will inspire our audience to look beyond current paradigms to challenge the issues of the future and to contribute to an effective and positive culture'.

I will therefore begin with an apology to those in this audience, either present or on-line for taking this task a step further. I think, I hope, that what I have to say today is not just twenty minutes of 'grumpy old man' ramblings but is a collection of thoughts shared

in a conscientious belief that we all need to just stop for a moment. We need to take a breath. We need to challenge some of our most entrenched beliefs.

We need to reorganise commitments; we need to replace mantras. We need to do something different if we want our world and our lives to be better. These thoughts I will share today are probably not inimitable but haven't come from thin air. They're a conclusion that my life, and my world, was too full of things that shouldn't be there. I am sure this is the case for most of us.

Over the last twenty years or so a pattern evolved in my life where most days I would go to work and look after people who were trying to die in front of me and then I would end up in a management meeting later in the day, talking about something inconsequential. Something that no thinking person should waste time on. I'd go back to my office and deal with the day's hundred emails by deleting ninety per cent of them. I would go home and turn on the TV news and hear a politician run through some shallow data to draw a conclusion that made no sense but could be supported by a partially analysed, convenient subset of the numbers. I would see people treated badly in our community and wonder why no one said or did anything to stop that happening. I would see organisations I was meant to trust, like banks and hospitals, fall apart in shame when their business practices and dealings with people were exposed.

Was I depressed? Was I burnt out? Was I just not coping? Was I too sensitive? Did I simply need to accept the modern world? Did I need to care less and stop wanting to intellectualise the world? Was I the one with the problem?

Or just maybe, I had stumbled on something that made sense – that could be the beginning of a solution, this realisation that my life seemed too occupied with things that at best weren't needed and at worst were destructive or wrong. I had conviction that my thinking was heading in the right direction, but I needed to organise these thoughts into a framework that made sense to others. Maybe this thinking could resonate and be pertinent in the real world for other people. A private theory on what's wrong with the world is after all rather pointless.

So, what did I do? I walked and thought a lot in the botanic gardens near my home. The rhythm of walking seemed to soothe the urgency of my mental chase for solutions, and simpler thoughts began to emerge more easily. Patterns and connections started to make sense and I wrote these things down. My brain had always made me look for boxes to put things in and labels to attach. I needed to pull out the themes and common threads linking what I believed was at the core of the wrongs in my world. I kept at it, and what began as obsession progressed to a more comfortable outflow of material that looked like it may become a way of understanding and resolving this issue of an overloaded life.

When I went back to any of those situations that triggered my discomfort or to that feeling of a need to solve a work or business or organisational or systems issue, I could provide myself with a simple piece of advice: remove that unnecessary impediment, task, process, or rule. Eliminate the unnecessary complication, the confected hurdle to jump, the bureaucratic speed hump, the time-wasters - just cut the crap.

Now that does sound like a grumpy and maybe arrogant old man, and you could be forgiven for dismissing my advice.

But let me explain ...

The 'crap' is not just what I choose to label crap, it's not just the things I don't like. It's an allegory for the collective pile of life's pollution, which encroaches on our space as humans. It can be a thing that occupies space, but is more likely to be a construct, a process, a rule, a cultural restriction, an action or an inaction of another. Perhaps it was just my way of thinking, but 'cut the crap' started to become a response for all those scenarios that detract from happiness or effectiveness characterised by lies, half-truths, meaningless process (we've always done it that way), duplication, waste, unnecessary complexity, lack of integrity, self-interest.

Is that response or reaction anything more than calling out something that an individual may think is not quite right? Or is it possible that such a simple profanity essentially represents a common gut-level retort to some of life's shit, which simply shouldn't be tolerated? Isn't it common to find that when we voice dissatisfaction, others join us in a chorus of shared recognition of some crap or other? Part of the 'crap' is the fact that not only do we individually and silently tolerate it every day, but that we build lives that use it as a foundation, and then we use it to cement our lives together.

Harvey paused for just a few seconds, which felt like much longer. He wasn't looking for impact from a pregnant pause; he just needed to see if he had reached the audience. He looked up at his single slide, projected to the right and left of the stage, and looked down at the front rows. He knew at once. The two or three half smiles of identification that he received when he returned the gaze of individuals – that was all he needed for now. He stepped out from the lectern to the centre of the stage a metre or so back from its edge and continued.

Colleagues, I would like to pose a simple question to each of you. We all encounter things in everyday life that trigger a feeling of 'seriously?' or 'what is this action/idea/situation doing in my world right now?'. Who in this audience has experienced something in the last week that has caused you to say to yourself 'seriously'? Who has stopped and realised that something they, or a colleague, were doing was a pure waste of time or resource? Who has heard a false or misleading statement or which, by employing a half-truth, has been uttered purely to persuade? Who has found themselves caught up in a process that is complex, but could be navigated much more simply than an existing system allows? I suspect the answer is that we all have had one or all of these experiences.

If we are happy to agree to some commonality, then what I want to spend the rest of this brief talk proposing is a handful of ideas to explain this thing I call 'crap' and to conclude with some thoughts on why we have allowed our lives to become so 'full of it'.

Pointing to the slide to his left, Harvey brought his laser pointer to 'challenge'.

Let's look at this first. CHALLENGE. As counterintuitive as it sounds, lack of challenge or confrontation is the starting point of much of our modern-day misery. How much of what is problematic in life is permitted to just float by without being challenged? What I mean by challenge here is the willingness that we should have to acknowledge openly and to act on the wrong deeds and wrong thoughts we encounter. Failing to do this is failing to acknowledge reality and failing to be honest about what we perceive.

We don't want to appear negative, we don't want to rock the boat, we don't want to upset the boss lest we miss the next bonus or promotion, we don't want to be perceived as someone who is not a team player; so, we don't confront issues. Sometimes we lack the confidence to say what we really think, and that lack of confidence allows wrongs to survive unchallenged. Sometimes we don't want to confront an issue because our lives are already too full and too complicated; we don't have the spare emotional energy it requires to take on a cause or to speak up. Sometimes we are sure of the negative response we will encounter so we lose our mojo.

Haven't we all encountered someone whose response to any request to look at something from another angle results in a predictable defensive shutdown. A response like: 'maybe the timing is not ideal', 'perhaps the organisation is not quite ready for a change like that', 'let's work on the change management around that idea'.

Many people see confrontation as something negative in the least and as something disrespectful or aggressive at most. But confrontation does not need to be these things – it can be simply a statement of the truth, rephrasing politically 'correct' language to truthfully describe an impact, and it can occur without threat. It is, in a pure sense, the exposition of an issue for consideration in a mature and objective way.

It may not necessarily result in a change in direction or outcome, but it does create the possibility of change. When we initiate constructive confrontation, we have at least been honest.

If we confront nothing, then nothing will change.

Harvey directed his laser pointer back to the slide and said: TRUTH.

The abuse of knowledge and distortion of the TRUTH is something that members of science-based professions have a real problem with. We see this too often and it drives us crazy, but we should feel some small comfort in realising that knowledge abuse is something that affects everyone.

In its most innocent form, abuse of the truth may be born of ignorance. An individual believes that measurement of a parameter proves a truth or describes reality. What they may not consider is the veracity and meaningfulness of the measure, or bias that may have led to the choice of that measure over another, or the potential impact of confounders and circumstance on that measure. They do not entertain the thought that their truth may not be the truth.

In its most unethical form, the abuse of knowledge may be the deliberate construction of a misleading measure or presentation of contrived data to further an agenda. Where I have talked about measurement, we can easily substitute the concepts of data, information, images, evidence, documentation or any other form of knowledge in our world.

As clinicians, we have all seen publication of so-called research where a clinical intervention is proposed by a group who will receive some benefit from a particular outcome. Bias has influenced a research question, subject enrolment may be prejudiced, data and outcome recording are often unverified or veracity is untested, and inconvenient outcomes are excluded on dubious grounds. Bias is also used in selective presentation of knowledge and we can see this any evening on our news broadcasts, where a politician, business person or protagonist for a cause will serve us a platter of carefully filtered half-truths and massaged information to demonstrate a point or sell a position.

By abuse of knowledge the wrong is to commit one of two sins (or maybe both).

The first sin is lack of objectivity and is without doubt the more common. How often do we hear something that has not been thought through objectively, where a proponent has at no point stood back and said, 'If someone else, without my preconceptions and biases were to look at this issue, would they reach the same conclusion I have?' Is this some form of intellectual laziness? 'I'm too lazy to think this through, so instead I'll run with the first reactive brain-fart that pops into my head'. Or is this behaviour more about not understanding the need for objectivity and a belief that a personal position albeit untested or unverified will suffice.

The second sin is misrepresentation of knowledge for personal gain or because of conflict of interest. Look no further than 'big-pharma' research outcomes, political polling and surveys, or a neatly edited (doctored) board report from a CEO with a performance problem. When is hiding information and presentation of half the truth a full lie? Haven't we all met this parsimonious approach to the truth in one form or another and thought to ourselves: 'Seriously, cut the crap – give us the full picture!'

To move on to another pile of crap, let me talk about wastefulness and the idea of SUFFICIENCY. Excess and waste are a problem of our lucky society and modern wealthy economies. The difference between these is subtle, but if we think about excess as an overproduction problem and waste as an inefficient usage problem, we get close to the mark. The obvious areas of excess and waste include such things as electrical power and fuel consumption, use of plastics, food wastage, irresponsible cropping, and livestock farming. We all recognise the issues of disposable everything, the fact that most of what we purchase (from the building we live in to the appliances we use) is constructed with a planned useful life at the end of which it will either be replaced by a 'necessary' upgrade or due to a technical failure… which we all know costs more to repair than does a replacement unit.

What we may not recognise so readily is the wastefulness and excess we build into our activities of everyday life. For example: Who needs to run a marathon? From a health perspective, no one needs to be fit enough to run a marathon, and many people have been injured or died in training or during a marathon. Surely the health benefits of fitness could be obtained by a person running five or ten or twenty kilometres. At the dichotomous extreme, why do so many people eat so much and exercise so little? We have created a world, lifestyles and cultures, which drive this.

But we also make individual choices.

Why do we over-fill our lives and our time with electronic gadgets? Don't get me wrong, I use and enjoy my computer, phone, TV and all the other paraphernalia. I do my work and research better because I have mastered IT tools and clinical electronic machines. But why do we allow email, social media, phones, tablets and all the rest to dominate our lives? Where does this form of excess come from and how do we resolve it? It is just crap that we've allowed to invade our lives, so perhaps we need to find a way to remove it, to cut that crap, to be comfortable with sufficient – not more.

Before moving on, let me pose another question about excess: 'Is the pursuit of perfection noble or wasteful? Is it excessive to set a mostly unattainable goal, the pursuit of which wastes resources?' Seemingly, I am proposing that usually a goal somewhere short of perfection is rational, is quite enough and is not associated with a waste of additional unrewarded effort and resource. Waste and excess are everywhere and in many forms.

In the same way, we have replaced SIMPLICITY in our lives with complexity as a form of crap, which wastes time, frustrates us and causes churning of effort and energy. Just consider bureaucracy – that special form of crap that should not be tolerated. A bureaucracy exists to administer and manage a system. Typically it's a collection of public sector employees who function at a level several stages removed from the operations they govern. They determine the rules that the system works by then determine rules for the creation of rules and process then administer those rules. They exist for and within the rules, not the services, and are so far removed from the services or outcomes that usually they lose sight of them altogether. Consequently, systems become increasingly convoluted and complex to the point of dysfunction. That's just a bit tragic if, for example, you happen to be a patient who needs a life-saving intervention that the bureaucracy determines can't be delivered this week because a rule says so – a form hasn't been filled out on time or the right committee hasn't met yet!

Sadly, there are many examples where we as individuals also increase the complexity of our own lives. In some respects, this is a modern plague of compulsion that we find it hard to avoid. We overfill our time and overcommit our emotional energy and suddenly find ourselves over-thinking and over-analysing the predicament we find ourselves in. To escape this, we need to accept a simpler view of our lives to frees us from the tangle of complexity – we make a sea change, a tree change, or down size, or de-clutter; we adopt an approach that suggests we shouldn't give a fuck. The commonality of all these approaches, which we find in the last chapter of a self-help book, is to reduce the complexity in our world and to enjoy the pleasure of simplicity.

At this point, Harvey turned to the slide projected to his right and highlights the words 'integrity and culture'. His mouth was dry. He was probably rambling. His thoughts were escaping without the usual filters but knew he was speaking with passion. Passion can smell a lot like zealotry, but right then he just needed to complete his message. He could worry about the reactions later.

There is a place inside each of us and in organisations that we work for or are a part of that is about INTEGRITY. We might call this something else: for me it may be my core values or an ethical construct that I live by; for an organisation it may be a culture or 'the way we do things around here', for others a life philosophy or religious belief. We can influence this inner-compass or culture by the way we live. Not surprisingly, some ways are more effective and better for our world than others. We need to see the empty cultures for what they are – part of the crap that we need to cut.

Much of our lives are spent interacting with organisations – from the local school to our workplace to the government. For all the talk, management strategy meetings, mission statements and planning-day outputs that we see, many organisations suffer from cultural insolvency. Commonly, there is an inability of an organisation to resource the development of a positive culture. These organisations flounder around and never seem to move forward. Their culture resists change, crushes innovation and drives the status quo. They support supporters of this culture and reject the rest. Often they do what is necessary to satisfy the masters, but if you take a close look, they will lack ethical robustness, commitment, diligence, proactiveness, professionalism, respect and diversity. They are not truly 'caring' organisations.

Sound like anywhere you know?

And the alternative?

Yes, a culture of integrity characterised by honesty, commitment, diligence, reliability, valuing others, caring about what we achieve. What makes some like this and others not? What makes this approach rub off on others? What makes whole organisations places of integrity. Perhaps empathy, perhaps compassion – I don't know for sure, but I do know that lack of integrity and lack of a positive culture is a palpable problem. It is too easy for us to lose sight of the impact that we have on others (and ourselves) and too easy to accept the failings and imperfections of our systems; but this form of weakness and apathy, this low-integrity culture is pathetic crap.

Harvey stands and moves across the stage resting his hand on the projection screen.

This last phrase: 'The magnetism of crap' – what do I mean by this?

The magnetism of this cluster of behaviours that lies at the core of much of our modern dysfunction is as addictive as sugar and meth, and as difficult to reject as these plagues. Many of our ills are due to over-attachment to ways of behaving, to the electronic tools we depend on for everything, to our need for success as defined by society. This is a reality that many of us find hard to understand. Why do we lock ourselves into these ways of behaving and living? What is the nature of this force, which we find impossible to resist? Is it a need to be part of something bigger or is it fear of missing out on something important? Where is the security we should be able to find in a simple life? The truth is that breaking the magnetism of our less-than-perfect existence is not much more complicated than prying apart two magnets – once they are separated their power is lost. We need to simply cut that basic bond.

Many of us humans are looking for something more in our world now – isn't that why we have burnout, substance abuse, workaholism, and why we don't look after ourselves physically, spiritually and mentally? Isn't that why we buy millions of copies of self-help books, cynically written to tap into this vacuum of emotional need?

I truly believe that the answer to this tragic guttural yearning is not so complex.

I have said we need to confront what needs to change. I have said we need to approach and apply knowledge with honesty. I have said we need to be prepared to resolve the unnecessary complexity of our worlds and to be happy with sufficient. I have said we need to frame these changes in a culture of integrity.

Finally, we need to understand and remove the attraction of this crap.

At each level all we need to do is identify and challenge ourselves to cut the crap. All the BS stuff that we allow to become the drivers of life, things we accept as given, but which are often constructs driven by a profit, markets, wrong thought or ill consideration. All the things we know at first blush are too complex, contrived, misleading, unnecessary. We need to see them, call them for what they are, confront them and their merchants and walk away from them. There is a finer way, a more sustainable and happier way to live, but to experience this we must develop the ability to take a different direction.

Harvey paused, this time for effect.

Thank you all for attending this session today and thank you for your attention. I apologise if you feel that these thoughts I have shared are all just a bit too abstract and need perhaps more illustration from the real world, however I hope that you will take the time to think simply about what I am proposing, and maybe one day another talk, a longer conversation and some shared thought could complete this story. In the meantime, Take the time to quietly or even silently allow yourself to 'cut the crap' when the time is right.

At a critical care conference, the audience rarely reacts and is almost never emotional. Unlike a virtuoso concert, a performance at these conferences would receive polite applause and some probing questions, seeking detail or justification. So Harvey was surprised when the applause just seemed to go on and on and was embarrassed when a handful of people in the audience stood in appreciation.

He had developed confidence in the material during its preparation and in the weeks before the conference when he'd rehearsed and edited it so many times. Still, he'd expected a polite, restrained response. Not this.

Chapter 4

Congratulations

In the coffee break after his session, Harvey was approached from every angle. No doubt there were some in the audience who either didn't get it, didn't agree or weren't overly impressed with his presentation, but there were many, many others. These friends, acquaintances or complete strangers gathered around him or approached the cluster he was now the centre of, hovering for an opportunity to pass on a word of congratulation or to shake his hand.

An ICU Director from Vancouver, who Harvey knew from a research collaboration group, approached him.

'Hello Mike,' said Harvey, 'good to see you here.'

'Very cool talk,' he said, 'though I did wonder if I'd booked in to a religious convention rather than a critical care conference.'

Harvey bristled a little but tried not to let it show.

'I'm pulling your leg, pal. It made me think.'

Danny Christopher, an emergency physician and critical-care retrieval specialist from New Zealand cut in.

'Harvey, I loved it. You know just last week I had an intensivist from Christchurch put me through the wringer in a retrieval case we were bringing up from the middle of nowhere; wouldn't take the patient till we had some authority form filled out for the billing. I ended up telling him to 'fuck off' and spoke to his boss – but a simple 'cut the crap' would have done the job. Those kinds of situations are nearly always full of the crap you are talking about. Well done, Harvey, I hope the people that need to get the message hear your talk!'

Harvey turned to his left, almost spilling his coffee as he bumped into a hovering Sandra Herriot from Oxford.

'Professor Pearce,' she said 'thank you for your talk. It was so topical. I feel like twenty minutes was barely long enough for you to present a table of contents of your ideas, but it made me think. We have an open session tomorrow on end-of-life care and limitation of treatment situations – I wondered if you would come and join our panel. Your ideas around sufficiency and honesty would resonate in that session – we see so much over-treatment and masking the truth of our clinical expectations in patients with terminal problems. Would you be free at 1.30pm for an hour or so?'

Harvey had delivered talks in the past that had introduced important clinical changes, radical improvements to systems and challenged old ways of delivering health care but had never been the focus of a reaction like this.

The connections were meaningful and came from parts of these clinicians that were personal and deep-rooted.

―⋎⋏⋎⋏―⋎⋏―

The bell rang. People moved to the next conference session like streams of ants heading to six different feeding locations around The Square. There were many concurrent presentations or workshops running at this knowledge banquet, so at least several hundred delegates would attend each meeting room or lecture theatre.

'Professor Pearce?' asked the uniformed conference concierge.

'Yes, that's me,' replied Harvey.

'Professor, would you be able to spend a little time with the media group on Level Two? Your presentation has them a bit excited and we a have mix of TV and newspaper reporters who would like to ask you a few questions. To be honest most of what they get access to here is quite technical and complicated research presentations, so they're always on the lookout for news about the next new life-saving intensive care intervention or something to do with disasters or military medicine or other material which appeals to the general public. Your talk seems to have them buzzing.'

'Sure, no problem. I'll be with you in a moment.' Harvey was a well-polished press performer, though he wouldn't say he enjoyed it. Reducing ideas and findings of research from five or ten-thousand-word paper to twenty second interview responses or three sentence quotes for a newspaper wasn't always easy.

At the top of the escalators on level two was a glass-walled mezzanine. The backdrop of old Brussels with its towers and spires framed the outlook in a cultured academic flavour. Waiting for Harvey was a group of at least fifteen media – reporters, camera operators, photographers, tech assistants. The conference media liaison officer ushered Harvey to the corner of the space and adjusted the left lapel on his jacket fixing one of those clothing malfunctions which would have had him looking like the caricature of the slightly-ruffled academic type. He thought he probably should have had a haircut. Too late.

Thirty minutes later the discomfort was over and Harvey was removing the lapel mic when he noticed a lingering member of the press group, a forty-something stylish woman keen to continue the interview.

'Professor Pearce, my name is Elli Clemence and I work for a group called Loquitur. Could I steal another moment of your time?'

'Yes of course, and please, it's Harvey.' He moved away from the dwindling throng.

Harvey knew of Loquitur, a production company who did some publishing, conferences and media products. In fact, one of his colleagues from Harvard had been approached by them to give a series of talks just last year. So, Ms Clemence was not a reporter but had come along to the media scrum. Interesting.

'Can I get you a coffee or something? You look like you probably could do with a break.'

Natural Café was one of those perfect city cafes where jetlagged or bored conference attendees could quickly escape to a seat in the sun with brain-shocking coffee or maybe something stronger later in the day. Harvey stirred the half sugar into his Earl Grey and wondered where this conversation was going.

'I enjoyed your talk,' said Elli.

'Well thank you.' Harvey smiled. 'I was keen to present something different for the Vincent, but to tell the truth, I wasn't really confident about this one.'

'What do you mean?'

'In twenty minutes I didn't really have time to take it beyond a very high-level talk –to bring it back to earth with all the real-world examples that ignited those thoughts. You know, it was all a bit philosophical – a pile of personal reflection and contemplation. Always risky.'

'Then why did you go there?'

'I've reached the point of too much irritation with the challenges in life, enough insight into the reasons for that and some ideas around solutions that seemed to hang together. You know, it just seemed right to share some of those thoughts. And then there's the invitation you get with this colloquium – the organisers make it quite clear they aren't after just another retrospective from someone at the rear end of their career. It makes you think.'

'Then your ideas … they aren't just thought bubbles for the colloquium? You really believe that the solution to life's problems is to just cut the crap?'

'Yep,' Harvey said. He couldn't put it more plainly than that.

'Harvey, I'm not sure if you know but Loquitur is now the biggest podcast producer in the medical world. I'm here in Brussels because we always get a handful of productions out of this conference, which really hit the mark with clinicians around the world. Seeing the presenter deliver their work in front of an audience always gives me a better idea of their potential as a podcaster and especially gives me a feel for the presenter's style, engagement, pizazz…. you know a flat podcast is a form of torture only outdone by a flat TED talk! I really enjoyed what you had to say and the way you delivered it this morning.'

'And…' lead Harvey.

'More a 'but' than an 'and' … Harvey, I agree that what you presented today has a lot of detail and complexity and connection to our every day that you didn't touch. Although your talk today was profound and provocative, the 'but' is that it needs those other conversations and detail to complete the story. Today you delivered a wakeup message. People everywhere will be interested in what you are saying and I don't just mean your ICU and Emergency friends. The 'but' is that I think you just presented the introduction, and I'm offering you the chance to develop and deliver the rest of the story with Loquitur over a podcast series.'

'OK.' Harvey tried to take that in. 'You're right, there is a lot behind what I presented today. I've been working on this for a couple of months on and off and, yes, I'd be interested. I return to Sydney at the end of the week and planned to start putting this material down on paper properly – maybe bring it together in a couple of perspective articles for a journal. I'm back on clinical rotation next week and

I've got a week of nights then three weeks of solid ED shifts coming up. Not very conducive to starting a project.'

'Starting the work with a series of podcasts may just be a manageable way to progress this,' said Elli. 'We've had several authors take a series of podcasts and evolve them into a paper or a publication – think of it as a way of distilling your ideas.'

Harvey thought on it. 'The idea of doing this as podcasts is attractive and surely is a change from writing this up as a paper to publish. It's a bit exciting and could give me a process and deadlines that I can work to… so, OK Elli, tell me how this would work.'

Half an hour later, Harvey understood most of what he needed to. He had agreed to read the material Elli would send by email later in the day and to get back to her with a final decision by the end of the week when he was due to fly home.

So, with a 'thanks for the tea', Harvey walked off to wander the symmetrical arrangement of paths in the Parc de Bruxelles. Deep in racing thought, a little animated and a little apprehensive, he walked down the perimeter, across the diagonal, around the fountain. Then again and again excited that these ideas could become something more useful, could mean something more…

He missed the rest of the conference that day and was, at best, half engaged with the rest of the presentations that week.

Chapter 5

Six Weeks Later – Sydney

Pearce vs Massey was a regular scheduled event on the tennis courts at Falcon Park, and Harvey nearly always arrived first, and early.

Today, Rob waited and killed time checking email and his collection of social media feeds on his phone – as usual, none of these added anything significant to his existence. The phone also told him it was 9.30 am Saturday 4 May 2019, sunny and twenty-one degrees. All correct and useful information, but where was Harvey? No answer to his call, no return of SMS and late by half an hour. Unheard of.

Rob walked the few hundred metres and up through the gardens to Harvey's home, tossing possible explanations around. The text message he received from Harvey late yesterday from Lamaro's suggested he was heading down the neck of a bottle. With the press releases yesterday and recent hassles at work, Rob wasn't surprised that Harvey took the afternoon off to chill. Eventually he settled on an expectation of finding him hung-over, incapable and amnestic of their 9am arrangement.

Harvey's front door was slightly ajar so Rob assumed he was about to appear and drag his sorry self down to the courts to be well beaten.

The house was quiet. Rob called out to Harvey, pressed the doorbell and let himself in. There was no answer from within so he wandered through to the lounge then out onto the terrace. He checked the garden and down the side of the house, where Harvey often spent time tending his vegetable patch. Nothing. As he scratched his head and walked back toward the terrace door, he glanced through the adjacent bedroom window and spotted Harvey lying on his bed. He knocked on the glass. 'Get up you lazy turd,' he called as he headed back inside.

Rob knew as soon as he entered the bedroom. Harvey didn't answer, and he never would. He wouldn't move, wouldn't react, would never again say anything.

Harvey lay there in his clothes – pale, cold, motionless. Gone.

For all his fifteen paramedic years, Rob always had the same quick and disturbing visceral response when he came across a dead person. That prickling of hairs on his neck, that slight start, a shudder deep inside. Death delivered a message of confronting finality which he found innately disquieting.

But here in Harvey's home, he felt nothing at all. No emotional tsunami for a virtuous friend he understood and respected and loved. Instead, a disturbing composure and detachment.

'No,' was all that Rob could say, as he started to take in the scene in front of him.

IV fluid hung from the bed-head, Propofol ampoules and packets neatly left on the bedside table, a canula in his left arm. The IV had run through completely. It all looked orderly, peaceful, serene… Surreal.

You bastard, thought Rob, there was no chance you were getting this wrong was there.

His friend was pulseless, apnoeic, lifeless – the waxy chill and firmness of the well-dead. He called 000 and waited. There was nothing for him to do. The EMS came, the police and the Coroner in turn.

He knew all the procedures and what to expect of each of the professional groups who came and plied the relevant parts of their trade for Harvey. All the same, Rob felt like he was on a movie set and it wasn't till Jess answered his call and came around that he began to feel.

A week later, Rob surprised himself and was able to speak at the funeral service – 'coherently and without emotional decompensation' as he called it. He acknowledged the honour of being Harvey's best friend and spoke of the pain that this loss had started to unleash inside him. He chose his words with care and addressed his eulogy to Harvey's only relative, his sister Charlotte.

'To have known Harvey was to have experienced an advantage in life. He was a man who chose to contribute to the world in all he did, a man of high ethical and moral standards. Sometimes those standards created a burden, which Harvey embraced and managed.

He was a man who loved life and work and lived fully, generously.

It is never easy to say goodbye to a friend, and when a friend leaves the world so early, and in this way, we are left with many questions and maybe a little anger and frustration to add to our sadness. That is OK. It's the way Harvey would have reacted.

He would know this is impossible to make sense of and would have understood our discomfort. He would know that we'd all ask 'Why?' and 'What could we have done?', because he would have asked those questions too. He would also have known we could never find a satisfactory answer to those questions. Despite this, we must all find a way to accept this unacceptable conundrum.

He would also have lectured us in his Chardonnay-Buddhist way about the likelihood of a 'something' beyond now. Yes, he has died – we all know that ... but perhaps we can also agree that if this is all there is to life, then our lives amount to a terrible waste of a lot of experience, love and spirit.

So, whether you believe in a god or a buddha or are simply romantic, it's hard to ignore Harvey's conviction that physical death is the beginning of something more, or perhaps the next step in the completion of something not yet finished.

Whether that's true or not, I don't know, but I am certain Harvey's memory and spirit will live on with us and that the memory and impact of his friendship will stay with us all for our own lifetimes.

His messages and his wisdom will prevail and his passion, which was such a force, will be there as a model for us all.

So today, while we are here to say goodbye to Harvey, we should also say 'Thank you, Harvey. We have been most fortunate to have experienced your influence, inspiration, guidance, love and friendship in our lives'.

Chapter 6

Six Weeks Before - Leaving Brussels

Harvey groaned silently as the plane touched down at Sydney airport early on March 25. He'd been on the move for too many hours and was due at work in three. An early flight from Brussels to Doha had connected with a fourteen-hour flight to Sydney. The early start was a drag, but a reasonable feed and a flatbed in business had taken the edge off it. He shouldn't complain really and, if he did, it he'd unlikely generate sympathy from anyone. He had time to get home and drop his luggage, shower and get to his evening ED shift at Queens. It started at 3.00pm and would finish by midnight – after which, thanks to some Temazepam and time zone differences, Harvey was likely to sleep for ten hours.

His house was cold when he arrived home. He never quite trusted the timer controls on the central heating to behave while he was away. It would have been nice if there was a 'significant other' to provide a welcoming.

For some reason, maybe just lack of time, he'd never married. Harvey had cared for partners, had even loved some, but had never found things right enough or himself committed enough to take the next step. Unsurprisingly he'd been told he was married to his job, which is only slightly better than being told 'you are your job' or 'your job is you'. He didn't care much about this but was lonely sometimes.

He didn't have anyone now and hadn't completely recovered from his last relationship of six years, which died a slow death until it was buried almost two years ago. He was almost at the 'can't be bothered' stage, which he believed translates to: live in quiet hope, avoid introduction-to-an-old-friend events and don't bother with crap like dating sites. He had a work life that was crowded with people. Often the quiet solitude and escape of a single life was a blessing.

Harvey arrived at the ED with half an hour to spare. He dropped his papers at his desk and went to catch up with his director, Alex. Harvey was surprised to find him in the department. Alex had been back at work for two days after his recent AMI and was in the office for short days and a four-day week for the next month.

Harvey wrapped on the open door and went straight in. 'Hey Alex, how are you?'

Alex turned from his computer screen. 'Not bad, jetsetter… essentially, it's a shitty day and I'm trying to get out the door. My cardiologist is on my case, my dietician is trying to kill me slowly and home is just a tiny bit stressed if you know what I mean.

I've only been back here a couple of days and I'm still getting my head around everything. If I'm not home by 1.30pm, Laura will ring me, and if I pull out my laptop at home, she'll probably hit me over the head with it. I'm being tortured by people trying to improve my life.'

Harvey was sad for Alex. He was a great guy and a fantastic leader, but managing life, the real world and your own health is a different thing to running an ED. The former, Alex was not good at. The latter he handled like a maestro.

'What can I do to help?' asked Harvey. 'I'm well rested after my front-of-plane flight, sober and yours to command.'

'Harvey, what I really need you to do is pick up an urgent case review and debrief. I've rostered Josh on for your shift – you know he's the new guy from Brisbane – and I need you to look at this case from last night.' Alex turned the computer screen towards Harvey and pulled up the record. 'This is a clusterfuck of Swiss cheese.' Harvey knew this mixed metaphor, which Alex reserved for the most problematic scenarios. The combined clusterfuck with a reference to Professor James Reason's Swiss-cheese millennial model of accident causation (applied liberally in aviation and clinical medicine) always meant trouble.

By 5pm Harvey had been through the notes, reviewed the lab results and looked at the scans from the case of thirty-three-year-old JP, a software engineer, husband of DP, father of two-year-old twins, type one diabetic, now deceased due to said clusterfuck.

Harvey's mind went back to the case he had seen just last week in the ED, then tried to remember how many times he had seen something go off-track in the care of these complicated characters.

By 7pm he had spoken with Dr Jess Goldman, who was on call the night before as well as Dr PF (advanced Registrar on shift) and Nurse MK (primary nurse), AKA the clusterfuckers, collectively responsible for JP's demise. He made himself a coffee and sat down to write the outline of a report he knew Alex would need first thing tomorrow:

JP was a 33-year-old male, who presented to Queens ED @ 11.15pm, Saturday 23 March 2019. Presenting problem was diabetic ketoacidosis with significant altered conscious state in known Type 1 diabetic. Triaged category 1 to Resusc-Bay 3 with PF and MK assigned to primary care stat. JP had been unwell for four days with rapidly progressing pneumonia, despite treatment from his GP with appropriate antibiotics. His deterioration accelerated on Sunday; however, due to his wife's work shift on Sunday, he had been alone for most of the day and was found by his brother at 10.30pm on 23 March.

Initial assessment showed shock (BP 80/40, HR 155), gross dehydration and coma (GCS 5). Initial bloods and x-rays were run, an IV commenced and intubation performed by 12.05am on March 24.

First consult with JG occurred at 12.17am. Shock had not improved, Acidosis was worse and blood chemistry results weren't through yet. JG declined to return to the hospital to supervise the resusc and advised calling the ICU resident, getting 'a handle' on the acidosis and fluid status and continue care as per protocol.

At 12.22am, the notes record instructions by PF to prep for ICU transfer (increase sedation and ventilator settings) and to administer a sodium bicarbonate infusion to correct the acidosis. The dose prescribed was 100mEq for IV infusion over thirty minutes.

At 12.43am, with a bicarbonate infusion running, JP was taken to the elevator for transfer to ICU. As the doors closed, he went into cardiac arrest and by the time he was at ICU (12.50am) he was unable to be resuscitated despite prolonged (and reasonable) efforts.

Consideration of the case and setting has identified several errors to be addressed:
- Failure to provide adequate IV fluid resuscitation for shock – the patient needed at least an additional 1000ml infusion in first hour.
- Failure to obtain urgent electrolyte assessment.
- Failure of the consultant on call to return for supervision of a critical protocol patient. The registrar was 'advanced'; however, is new to department and hospital and is 'untested'.
- Failure to check the electrolytes result prior to bicarbonate administration. Potassium was low-normal range, suggesting severe risk in administration of bicarbonate.
- Unnecessary prescription of bicarbonate infusion – the pH was later found to be 7.05. (Bicarb should only be considered if pH is less than 6.9-7.0.)

- Incorrect dose of bicarbonate administered – the drug order was miscalculated and patient was administered 1000mEq (10-fold dose error).
- ICU transfer of critical patient while unstable. There was no urgency for transfer, which was hastened due to administrative pressure relating to a shift changeover in ICU.

In summary, the causative event leading to the death of JP is likely to have been a rapid fall in potassium, secondary to an inadvertent bicarbonate overdose, resulting in cardiac arrest.

Preliminary reviewer assessment of the root causes are as follows:
- Clinical assessment and prescribing errors appear to be practitioner performance breaches.
- Lack of appropriate supervision of trainee staff by consultant staff.
- Drug-dose preparation and administration errors are due to inadequate infrastructure and equipment systems.

Contributing factors are drawn from known historic underlying issues and additional case issues:
- Practitioner fatigue – excess night shift and extended shifts due to staffing deficits.
- Incomplete induction due to time pressures with resultant lack of familiarity with protocol and standards.
- Possible practitioner burnout issue leading to lack of engagement with the case – staff member leave is pending but awaits staff replacement strategy (yet to be approved at hospital executive level).
- Alternate contemporary technologies are available to guarantee safe drug administration – previously requested, however, budget unavailable as of February 2019.

Recommendations:
1. This preliminary review has identified potentially critical systems failures as directly contributing to patient death.
2. Notification of State Coroner – immediate case referral to the Coroner is required.
3. Notification of Health Department: This is a Severity 1 classification incident, where direct and serious patient harm has occurred. Reporting is mandatory.
4. Commencement of urgent local Root Cause Analysis.
5. Urgent Executive meeting is advised, to include CEO, ED Director, Divisional Director and Quality and Safety Lead, to implement immediate resource and mitigate the risk of a similar incident in the future.
6. Immediate briefing of hospital insurer and lawyers.
7. Staff interventions, including education and counselling.
8. Family meeting and open disclosure discussion. In my view it is imperative that we initiate a meeting with JP's family to explain what we can and to apologise for our appalling system failings and this inexcusable outcome.
9. As per standard incident review process, the Root Cause Analysis is to be formally performed by an interdisciplinary team within fourteen days.

—⋎⋏⋎⌐⋎⋏—

Harvey signed off the report and logged it in the departmental incident tracking software. The wave of nausea that followed had nothing to do with jetlag, and he sat silently for a minute while his brain screamed muted exasperation. Anyone else would punch a hole in the wall, he thought. He wondered if that would help?

Instead he knew he would be the 'always calm', 'we can work through a solution', measured and responsible chap that he was known to be.

Truthfully, a part of him wanted to yell at someone or break something.

Only a month ago Harvey had written to the hospital executive raising his concerns about almost identical issues and neither he nor Alex could get any traction in resolving a problem that was guaranteed to cause harm again. Any executive with an ounce of integrity could not have ignored the risks. What was obvious and tangible danger to the practitioners seemed unrecognisable to the game-players upstairs.

This time the patient had died. They now had a shroud to waive.

He finished up and headed home just after midnight. The night sky was clear, and a cool wind tried to clear his mind of the mounting anger that came with reviewing JP's death.

All the same, sleep would be difficult. The phone call with Alex tomorrow morning would be interesting.

Chapter 7

Tuesday 26 March 2019

Alex had barely hit the office when his phone rang and Harvey's number appeared on the screen.

'Hello Harvey.' Alex knew he sounded tired already.

'Hi Alex, I thought I'd better give you a call to follow up on the report I sent through last night. It's tragic stuff. Have you got a moment now?' Harvey said.

'Sure, fire away, but before you get going you need to know I got an email from Jess Goldman last night. She wanted to know if I expected her to stand down immediately.'

'That's crazy, Alex, we know she's not well. She's not responsible for this and shouldn't wear it. She was upset last night after I went through the case with her, but we agreed to catch up today and talk through it some more. Let me talk to her this morning and I'll get back to you.'

'OK but go gently.'

'Sure. Look, regarding my report, I think this case is going to explode. The errors are plain and the background systems stuff is as obvious as dog's balls. This reads like a rehash of my last report and I don't see anywhere for the hospital or health department to hide on this. The real question is whether we need to take independent action.'

'What exactly do you mean, Harvey?'

'Alex, I'm concerned that we'll submit this report and just get another nothing response. Have you had a chance to look at it?'

'Yes, this morning and I agree with your conclusions and recommendations. I know it's a risk that we'll get little response, but we still need to follow process and I wouldn't be taking this externally right now. I'll send it up the line with an urgent flag and call upstairs later this morning. The CEO will get briefed and we should get a response by the time you get in this afternoon. I'll let you know where we get to. And you get back to me after you catch up with Jess.'

'OK, Alex. Sorry to drop this on you. You OK?'

'Yup – talk later'. Alex rang off.

By 10.15am, Harvey had done his gentle six-kilometre circuit around the botanical gardens and was on his way down to RockBar on the Harbour to meet up with Jess Goldman, grab a coffee and walk the waterfront path if the autumn rain and wind had settled. After drinking his coffee and watching hers get cold, Harvey called Jess. He was certain they'd said 10.15am. When she didn't answer, he shifted his thinking from mildly irritated to mildly worried. He left a message and headed off – perhaps his jet-lag was worse than he thought. He would follow up with her this afternoon before he went into work if she didn't call in the meantime.

Afterwards, Harvey packed up and headed in to work. He didn't start till 3 but needed to finish his discussion with Alex and wanted to clear his desk before his clinical shift that evening. He hadn't worked a shift on the floor for a couple of weeks and was keen to get back in, see some patients and have the ED ticking over smoothly. That part of the job was always satisfying especially when he actually got to provide some one-on-one care. Jess still hadn't replied so he followed up with an SMS and drove down to Queens.

Before he had time to sit down Alex's head appeared in the doorway, and the rest of him followed it into the office.

'Are you tracking me?' quipped Harvey

'Sorry Harvey, you're in early today. I'm not stalking you, but I wanted to catch up before you hear from someone else… '

'Hear what, Alex?'

'I had a call from the Emmanuel Intensive Care Director. Jess is with them. She was admitted last night after an OD. She's stable, Harvey.'

Harvey's face must have said it all. Alex continued. 'Look, she's going to be OK. She was brittle and I guess the case from Sunday was enough to tip her, but whatever; Rob found her when he got home and he rang 000. She was in Emmanuel ED inside thirty minutes and was never in danger. I don't think she was suicidal, but the unit at Emmanuel will deal with that. Rob said that she wanted you to know this wasn't about you or the review discussion yesterday.'

Harvey knew that was at best a half truth and felt sure that their discussion may well have been what tipped Jess. He thought for a moment and couldn't decide if he was sad, angry, guilty or just totally despondent.

'Fuck this Alex. I spent two hours yesterday going through that case from Sunday, and every minute of it made me more pissed off. Jess is caught here in the middle of a situation we all knew was on the horizon and now she's as much a victim as the guy who died. A month ago, we had a clear story about resource deficiencies and holes in the system, which we presented to all the right people and got no action. Now we have a dead patient, a sick doctor and who knows how many damaged people spread around the guy's family and our staff. Alex, we've been over this ad nauseam and we know what's needed: more staff, more money, more admin time for our lead doctors and nurses, and for fuck's sake some reasonable access to beds so the ED patients get off a trolley and into a ward before they die lined up in our over-crowded corridors.'

Alex was not a small man, and his jowly southern Italian looks were accentuated by dark fleshy sacs below his eyes and a sallow not-enough-sleep complexion.

'I know all that Harvey and I've got some time with the CEO and Board Chair later today, so let's see how that goes. Failing that, maybe the idea of some 'external discussion' may be worthwhile. There's always the health department whistle-blowing option. Leave it with me and we'll talk tomorrow. By the way, thanks for doing the review. It's spot on.'

Harvey waited for Alex to leave, made himself a coffee and flipped open his computer. He was sure he'd find a couple of hundred emails worthy of his delete button. There, fifth from the top of his inbox was one from Elli Clemence, with just a one-liner asking him to give her a call. The message made him stop and think about Brussels and his talk. Hadn't he just landed in a 'cut the crap' moment here at Queens. All this just reeked of lies and cover-ups, system failures, and lack of integrity. Maybe he needed to add that to his talk: 'developing awareness of the crap around you before you drown in it'. He had some time to kill before his shift started, so he rang Elli's mobile number.

Harvey had replied to her email on the weekend before returning to Sydney telling Elli that he was interested in doing the podcasts she had proposed. She let him know she'd talk with her producer about the idea and get back to him.

They chatted for a while, clarified a couple of issues about recordings and file transfers, till Elli finished with a cheery, 'Thanks again, Harvey and congratulations. This is a huge opportunity. Let's talk later in the week and don't forget to get the contract back to me.'

Half an hour ago, Harvey had been growling in anger and frustration and now he should be happy about a fantastic opportunity landed in his lap. Too much for one day, he found the high and low cancelling each other. The effect was that he experienced nothing special.

Shelving his thinking, he walked out into the ED and resusc room. Much better to just deal with the real world, he thought to himself.

Clemence's offer had been clear. Her producer and the development team at Loquitur had been impressed by Harvey's passionate and slightly irreverent presentation, and were offering a contract for a 'Cut the Crap' series of six, twenty-minute episodes over eight weeks, starting next month. For the first intro episode they planned to use his Brussels colloquium with some polishing and re-recording, and for the other five, they wanted him to develop his key messages: Truth, Sufficiency, Simplicity, Challenge and Integrity. Harvey didn't really need to think about it and would send the signed contract back to Elli tomorrow. He could re-do Brussels next weekend and figured spitting out the rest over the weekends in April and May without too much trouble.

—⋏⋏—⋏⋏—

Meanwhile, the real-world shit had hit the fan in the ED and Harvey was on the run. The guy in resusc was trying to die with an acute myocardial infarction and needed to get to the cath lab now, the kid the EMS had just brought in almost certainly had meningitis and needed an IV and antibiotics sooner than now, the fracture in the Injury Room needed a procedure in the next 30 minutes to avoid vascular compromise and a dead arm. Just a routine shift really. He loved it.

Time flew by and, for a while, he escaped thoughts of dead thirty-three year olds and organisational failure.

By 10.45pm, the department had started to settle; some notes needed to be written, a couple of tests ordered then he hand over to the night staff. It'd been a good shift. Body count zero and several 'thankyous'. His mobile rang. Harvey picked up the call from Alex.

'Harvey, I'm sorry to disturb, but I need to share some joy.'

Harvey wandered out towards the tearoom where he could talk more comfortably.

'I won't be in tomorrow and will need you to keep an eye on things. The meeting this afternoon didn't go well and I need to escape for a day or two – I don't need this now and suspect my cardiologist will agree! The Board Chair didn't turn up to our meeting and the CEO was arse-covering and pointing blame in every direction except his own. Bottom line: he maintains there is no issue with resourcing or the hospital's systems. Apparently, the issue is with us – leadership and culture – and our management of clinical standards in the ED. What a joke. He's told me he's going to announce an external review of the department to start next week and, as far as he's concerned, the JP case can get managed by the hospital Quality Case Review team 'in the fullness of time'. He's got no intention of escalating it or reporting it through to the health department.'

'Hold on.' By the time Alex was finished, Harvey was furious. 'That was a clear level 1 incident, which means we have a mandatory obligation to report it to the Health Department Safety and Quality Unit. Hutten doesn't get the option to sit on that sort of case. If a health service causes a patient death there's no option. We have to report to the Coroner and the Department, and we have to do a Root Cause Analysis within thirty days.'

'I know, I know,' replied a worn Alex. 'At this stage though their strategy is to gag us and reverse the blow torch with a review of non-existent 'issues'. It's a classic manoeuvre, which will find nothing, cost a lot and delay long enough to extinguish the belly fires – and we all stop agitating.'

'Classic,' said Harvey. 'Let's blame the victims and find a way to hide the bodies. Don't worry, Alex, I'll mind the fort and you take the time you need. I'll stay in touch. Night'

'Good night, Harvey, and thanks, pal.' Alex rang off.

Harvey didn't think his boss had ever called him 'pal' before.

Chapter 8

Cut the Crap – TRUTH

Harvey spent most of the next two days covering routine management business for Alex. He was busy and had no time to turn his mind to his report and the shelving it'd received. Somehow the week muddled on and Harvey arrived at Friday night with a bottle of red and a pizza. Pure panacea.

He completed the therapeutic milieu with the open fire, a movie themes playlist and his favourite armchair then settled down to finish the book he'd picked up at Brussels airport. Harvey had been in one of those slightly melancholic, deep-thinking solo-traveller moods after the conference, so had picked up a book from the 'personal development' shelves – snappy title, bright cover-blurb, lots to offer. The first two chapters had been promising. The recipe is simple: a couple of gratuitous concepts, which naturally resonate with ninety per cent of the population provides the reader with affirmation that they were on the right track in solving their woes. Instant connection with the author so they read on until by chapter six you realise that this is just another waffle book spouting pseudoscience and platitudes. 'Cut the crap,' he thought to himself, not missing the irony of this and the writing he had lined up for the weekend.

He put it down and reached for a Stephen King, which had been sitting on the side table patiently waiting for him to get to it. Now there's a proper book.

Harvey had a quiet weekend ahead. He needed to finish the re-do of Brussels for Elli and would work on the draft of the 'Truth' podcast.

Hello all. I'm Harvey Pearce. In real life I work as an Emergency Physician but in this handful of podcasts I'm sharing a series of ideas and an approach to our modern world that I hope will make a difference. What I'm challenging people to do is simply be brave enough to 'Cut the Crap' from life and enjoy a happier existence. This isn't medicine or research; it isn't religion; it isn't the self-help industry. It's just you, your life and permission to call out and drop what you know is the garbage inherent in your corner of today's world.

In a recent talk I gave in Brussels, I said that when I went back to any of those many situations that triggered discomfort or to that feeling of a need to solve a work, business, organisational or systems issue, I would usually end up providing myself with a simple piece of advice: just cut the crap. This usually means that someone else is contributing crap to my world. Sometimes it's just me!

'Crap' is not just the things I don't like. It's an allegory for the collective pile of life-pollution encroaching on our space as humans – so it can be a thing that occupies space or is more likely to be a construct, a process, an action or an inaction of another. Perhaps it was just my way of thinking, but 'cut the crap' started to become a response for all those scenarios that detract from happiness or effectiveness and are characterised by lies, half-truths, meaningless process (we've always done it that way), duplication, waste, unnecessary complexity, lack of integrity, self-interest.

Today I'm going to explore this from the perspective of the truth and of the abuse and misuse of knowledge. So, get comfortable, open your mind and (hopefully) enjoy!

Truth.

Truth is the expression of fact or reality, and to establish fact or reality we require knowledge. Knowledge is simply the sum of information we have access to.

To me it seems reasonable to say that it is right to use knowledge that is correct and complete, and to present it in a balanced and fair way. So, it follows that we wouldn't use knowledge that is known to be incorrect. We don't present half the truth (which is only a convenient part of the sum). And we don't dress the knowledge just to impress or influence. We present data in a way that contributes to the information that others may augment and thereby we construct knowledge.

Abuse of knowledge is the construction of something less than this in the form of misunderstanding, misuse or mischief. Misunderstanding may come through ignorance or intellectual naiveté. Misuse is the partial or selective misrepresentation of knowledge. Mischief is the straight-out presentation of untruths.

Next I'd like to consider why people abuse knowledge and then discuss the impacts this abuse may have.

Why do we abuse knowledge?

Probably the most usual form of knowledge abuse arises from where we source information. This may simply be a matter of not appreciating or understanding that a piece of information is incorrect or perhaps not appreciating the impact of incorrect knowledge. In some cases, this may be a form of intellectual naiveté. There is often no particular ulterior motive, no agenda. This may be a matter of intellectual irresponsibility or of intellectual laziness – not looking for reliable information and knowledge. Instead simply espousing opinion (informed or otherwise) is all too easy in the era of blogs, posts and tweets. Presenting an opinion of one person as definitive knowledge is an interesting concept isn't it? Especially if they have the right platform!

Considering another perspective: how often do we accept that what we see in the newspaper, Facebook or TV must be correct, just because it is there? Why do we believe that we don't need to test the veracity of it? Why do we accept that this is the way we get information or knowledge?

As human beings we are both fallible and corruptible and a generic form of corrupted judgment that interferes with the truth is bias. I could provide you with a definition of bias that a researcher or a statistician would be proud of, but in an everyday sense, it is simply a failure of objectivity. Objectivity in the establishment of knowledge extends from the validity of the items we choose to measure through to the precise way we measure or evaluate them. Of course, we can have bias, which is simply an innocent error in the way we are thinking, because few of us are perfect thinkers. On the other hand, bias can be, and quite often is, completely intentional.

Without thinking, we apply bias – the old 'it worked well when I did xyz last time or in a previous job' may be just a form of learning and application of life's lessons or it may be a form of bias transported from one experience to another. It may be innocent or it may be mischievous.

When we act out of self-interest, we abuse knowledge in a more sinister and calculated way. In the situation where we have a real or potential conflict of interest and do not responsibly manage that, the knowledge we have becomes an instrument of wrongdoing. Clearly, conflict of interest may lead to an unexpected and uncalculated bias, but it may also lead to a pathway of deliberate lies, corruption and exploitation.

The point is: all these reasons for misuse of knowledge, of tampering with all or parts of the truth just lead to presentation of crap information as knowledge. We need to accept that this is not OK, not 'just a feature of human behaviour' or in some way tolerable. It is, in reality, just crap.

So, what forms does this knowledge abuse or truth-tampering take?

The pervasive use of knowledge of convenience is an everyday happening, in that people just use the knowledge that supports their position. From the salesperson espousing a planet-saving energy-management feature of a new car to the politician quoting a poll from his local constituency, the game is the same.

If the car salesperson added the fact that the energy saving features were measured in an experimental setting that could at best be reproduced in 10% of everyday driving experience…

If the politician added that the poll was obtained by telephone, thereby cutting a whole segment of the socio-economic pie (those too poor to own phones)…

This partial presentation of information will inevitably lead to incorrect beliefs and that's not OK. In these examples there is manipulation of the knowledge produced by enquiry. A more ominous form of knowledge manipulation is entirely possible when there is deliberate misrepresentation of correct knowledge.

This can be as simple as omitting consideration of information we know to be correct, but which does not support a position the proponent is arguing. It can be as complex as reworking data with statistical and other tools to exclude the 'inconvenient data' or to recalculate data in a way that supports a preferred position. It can be the straight-out burying or suppression of knowledge.

Health research abounds with published findings that are unsupportive of change and contradict earlier research. How can this be – research that seems to prove something and later research that disproves the same thing? Some years back a neurologist friend presented a paper at Saint Elsewhere Hospital's research meeting. In that paper, he talked through a half dozen published papers released subsequent to some primary research and which did not reproduce the findings of the 'game-changing' primary research. He then went on to show in another half dozen papers how a 'not unreasonable' rework of the statistics in these papers invalidated results that had led to change in practice or use of a new drug. Now, lots of people have given talks about the potential for dubious findings and conclusions in medical (and especially drug) research. At the end of his talk in the Q&A session he was asked by the Director of Research 'why had he presented such a cynical and negative view of research and it's motivations?' In other words, wouldn't it have been better to suppress this view of the flawed knowledge? In case you feel this is a harsh criticism of the research director's question, the same director approached my friend after the session and privately 'advised' him that this kind of presentation was potentially damaging to research funding and the hospital's research prowess, as well as relationships with external national research bodies…

Less commonly, health practitioners will be presented with scenarios where things go wrong and their systems fail badly. There are many examples over recent decades – Bundaberg, Prince Edward Hospital, Bristol Royal Infirmary, which are well known. A common thread in each of these scenarios was suppression of the truth. Each hospital and its leaders knew it had a problem and many deaths and much harm could occur while administrators sat on and buried the truth, failing to report, failing to inquire, failing to fix. Suppression of the truth allowed them to temporarily hide from their responsibility for these failings and more importantly for the solutions. The same thing could be happening in your hospital and the tragedy is that knowledge is hidden for perverse reasons – knowledge that could save lives and prevent more suffering.

Why do I pick on health for this example? Isn't medicine a noble, healing, humanistic industry? Yes, it is, but principally at a personal or individual practitioner level. At the system level it is just another industry with all the corporate and financial drivers common to modern business. The point is that if knowledge abuse occurs like this in the arena of human wellbeing and health, isn't it disturbing to think what may happen when there is no humanistic consideration?

Another form of knowledge misuse to think about is the knowledge that we have gotten or constructed through 'overworking' an association. To use a banal example, research may show that people who live in large houses have longer life expectancy than those who live in small houses. Therefore this 'wrong knowledge' could suggest that if all poor people moved to larger houses they would live longer. The more rational interpretation of the research is that people who live in large houses have a socioeconomic advantage that affects health and well-being – perhaps through education, diet, access to healthcare and so on.

Every other day it seems the press report a piece of research in which causality is claimed from a simple statistical association – sometimes this is their naivety, but sometimes it is the researcher who milks the association to exaggerate the value of their research for personal gain.

Now I want to touch, briefly, on the knowledge-sin of over-emphasising apparently beneficial process improvements that have no effect on outcome. An example comes to mind from the world of paramedic research: a research project shows that paramedics can safely assess childhood asthma and administer injections of a corticosteroid. This research 'knowledge' is then applied, and paramedics start giving children injections of steroid. A later study surprisingly shows that when these children attend a hospital for management, there is no demonstrable difference in outcome. This is not because the treatment is ineffective; it is because the timing of the injection – in the ambulance or the ED – makes no difference.

The researcher did not investigate this aspect of the therapeutic intervention in the original research because they were (wrongly) more interested in a paramedic expanding their practice and administering a new treatment than they were in the child receiving an outcome benefit. The 'knowledge' was mistaken knowledge about the feasibility of a process and not an outcome; therefore, the introduction of the treatment (the process) was unnecessary and potentially diverted resources away from cases where the system might achieve outcome improvements.

We disguise much of the incorrect information that exists in our imperfect world through its intermingling with legitimate knowledge to create a new knowledge sum. The result is a new fact or belief based on a partly false premise. In the short term this may suit our purpose and may even be of benefit. In the longer term, it is likely to lead us astray. Eventually the knowledge error will be demonstrated when it is confronted by a challenge, interaction or question. Downstream this will add risk, complexity and rework. Why would we want to do that?

Look at this at the level of a large system. Most systems work as complicated organisms affected by many pieces of knowledge, sources of information and interacting processes. If knowledge is correct (true), then it is likely that we will get things right in design of the knowledge-dependent system. In the converse, if the knowledge is only superficially supported, but is at its heart wrong or incomplete or has not factored complex relationships and influences, then we may be in for a catastrophic surprise. This is the land of 'unexpected consequences' – a land we inevitably visit more often in a complex system. Ironically, if the knowledge that informs the design of a complex system is flawed, then unexpected consequences become inevitable. There is nothing new about the idea that interconnections abound in our world or that we are prone to unintended consequences. My point is that by eliminating crap knowledge or crap information we reduce the frequency of surprises.

Let me give you an example from my world in health again. For many years, crowding in emergency rooms has been an unpleasant fact in publicly funded health services. (Notably in private health services, the provider's response to the payer, who doesn't like to lie on a gurney in a hallway and will vote with their feet/dollars next time, is to solve the problem and get the patient into a bed in a sensible timeframe). Somewhere along the track, research showed that people staying greater than an arbitrary time in an emergency room had higher death rates during their later inpatient stay in hospital. Now this is obviously a simple association between time and death and doesn't explain why the association exists.

As a reaction to this and general complaint 'noise' many health systems introduced rules that patients must be admitted or discharged from the ED in a certain timeframe, usually four hours. It doesn't take Einstein to work out that for some patients this will be good (get into a bed faster, get definitive care faster, and presumably get better faster). It also doesn't take a genius to work out that for some patients this rule will result in premature or even unnecessary admission to hospital or discharge home because the outcome emphasis has changed from the treatment endpoint to the process endpoint.

This is a good example of using incomplete knowledge to drive a change in a complex process by which we create an unintended and unexpected impact. Had we worked with more complete information or more accurate knowledge, we would have been less likely to be tripped up and to create unintentional harm.

So, to wrap up…

Unfortunately, the fact that we may generate furious and righteous agreement about the need to cut this crap doesn't mean that achieving our goal will be easy. However, a starting point is the ability to see wrong or incomplete knowledge and deviation from the truth as a challenge.

The challenge is to look at the full picture always, deal with knowledge with objectivity, test our preconceptions and personal biases and acknowledge incomplete information.

Working with and committing to knowledge and the truth is important to the strategies and thoughts that will follow in the rest of this series of podcasts.

For now, the bottom line is that by elimination of incorrect information (cutting that crap) we come closer to the truth. Doesn't this make sense? Isn't this a reasonable goal?

By the time he pressed the send button on his draft for Elli, Harvey felt drained. Fortunately, his bottle of Shiraz was not, and he turned back to this friend.

This writing was different to authoring a paper or a chapter or preparing a lecture for his students. Sure, it lacked some of the discipline he applied to those writings, no footnotes or references, but this material came from deep inside him and exposed some of himself. As he sat, he thought back to the report he wrote only days ago. Was allowing it to be suppressed as bad as actively suppressing it? Although much of what he had written about truth was in the abstract, unveiling examples that carried huge burdens of harm to people was part of that exercise. Confronting.

This came with a degree of compromise of his private self and left him feeling deflated, despite a conviction that his thoughts and ideas would resonate with many.

Chapter 9

Sunday 31 March 2019

Sundays were for recovery and, when he wasn't on shift, Harvey religiously started the day with a game of tennis. He had a few regular opponents and today's foe was Jess Goldman's long-time beau, Rob Massey. Rob and Harvey went back a few years, having crossed paths at various times. Rob was now a senior paramedic in the local critical care and rescue team and consistently delivered extremely sick people to Queens ED. That's where he and Jess had met, a long time before Harvey moved to Sydney. Paramedic 'pairing' was common amongst emergency physicians and Jess had easily and permanently fallen for Rob and vice versa.

Harvey hadn't spoken with Rob since Jess had been admitted to Emmanuel last week but had received a text from him confirming their standing arrangement for a couple of sets this morning. Jess had been discharged after just forty-eight hours and Harvey hoped that she would turn up with Rob this morning. She'd often come along and divide her attention between a book and watching the two gents slugging it out. Neither were in their prime, but both showed signs of serious skills and technique, residual from past prowess, tempered by slightly worn joints, and constrained by waning aerobic fitness. Rob was a reliably better performer and usually won the day, but Harvey gave him something to think about with his curly swinging left-hand serve and the nasty spin that left-handers often seem blessed with. He couldn't do up a button with his right hand, but put a stick or a club or a racquet in his left hand and he was a gun.

Harvey jogged down to the Falcon Park courts. It was only a short run through the gardens and some side streets, but it did make him feel more virtuous and did loosen up some of those muscles and joints that needed a stretch before he launched into US Open mode. The courts were a mixed bag of good and not-so-good, but he managed to get one of the refurbished ones. It was a beautiful spot, just above the rose garden only a week or two from the end of its annual bloom. A few bushes braved the cooler autumn nights and were still in flower.

Rob pulled into the car park as Harvey arrived. Jess was sitting in the passenger seat. Fearing an awkward encounter or worse, a difficult silence, Harvey opened the door for Jess. She got out and Harvey moved forward silently to give her a gentle hug, holding her for a little longer than a usual hello. He stepped back and noticed that eye glint, just a thought or a word away from a tear. He saw the Band-Aid on her wrist, confirming a recent IV site, and looked away before his gaze became conspicuous.

Harvey quietly said, 'Jess, I'm sorry about last week – I hope you're holding up.'

'I'm OK, Harvey. In fact, in a weird way this has helped us deal with some issues that needed attention.' She glanced at Rob picking up his racquet from the trunk. 'Let's chat after you boys do your thing together.'

Harvey was happy to sense both positivity and the humour coming from Jess and moved around the car to greet Rob. He placed a matey hand on Rob's shoulder before they headed off to the court.

Rob didn't have a lot to say and Harvey detected some tension; not surprising really. Jess and he were connected like few couples, instinctively sharing each other's' highs and lows. The last few weeks had been tough. Regardless, Rob was up for a good hit, and let fly, running Harvey around the court, serving like a champ and showing no mercy. They always played three sets, no matter the score. And today looked like Rob's day as he won the second set having done Harvey six-four in the first. Harvey surprised himself with a comeback in the third to win it six-one after Rob's concentration fell apart. He lost track of end changes and a couple of times went to serve from the wrong service court. If Harvey hadn't been tracking the score, he was sure Rob would have got that wrong also.

The three of them wandered down to Noshry in Domain Street for a coffee and a chat. Harvey and Rob demolished a bottle of water before the coffees arrived and praised each other in customary habit for their remarkable plays – both turning the agreed blind-eye to their less spectacular moments. They reached an inevitable and awkward silence that Jess broke.

'Harvey, you know last week, I wasn't trying to top myself.'

Although Harvey had assumed they would breach the sensitive topic, he wasn't expecting quite such a blunt leap in. His face must have registered his surprise. Jess continued.

'I know my pharmacology extremely well, Harvey, and if I wanted to die, I think I would have been able to make that happen. The truth is that after our chat about that case last week, I had a couple of drinks and muddled my meds. I dropped off in front of the TV and woke up a couple of hours later unable to remember if I'd taken them. It was bizarre and I was super uptight. I was kind of on autopilot and took more – I don't know exactly how many, but with that and the booze, I was well out to it when Rob got home. He was worried, so I ended up at Emmanuel and the rest you know. There's nothing like that grinding anxiety and the restlessness and agitation that comes with a panic attack. I hadn't had one before, but the shrink at Emmanuel was definite about this episode.'

Jess sipped her coffee. 'The bit you don't know is exactly what has been happening over the last few months. I'm sorry I couldn't tell you all about it and a good dose of burnout seemed a plausible cover story!'

Rob touched Jess on the arm and turned to Harvey. 'This is more about me Harvey – Jess has been putting up with a shitload of stress that I've been bringing home. Things have been mounting up at work and now I feel like I'm stuck in a corner. It's become a big part of our world at home and Jess and I thought maybe you could give us some advice or help out. I'm sorry to do this to you, pal, but this is new ground for me.'

Harvey was concerned and curious, and felt a little flattered, so listened carefully for nearly thirty minutes as Rob told the story of his last three months.

'You know just before Christmas last year I was promoted to team leader for Division Three. Part of the job is the standard Divisional operational role. God, mate, I knew it would be full on… but it's the routine management for the east side ops, all the usual staff management, recruiting, performance management, right down to overseeing stock and drug management for the teams. The other part of the job, and presumably the reason I got it, is to oversee professional standards and to chair the service level performance and incident review committee.'

Rob leaned back slightly, his hands clasped behind his neck, and took a breath.

'So, I'm happy, Jess is happy. It's a promotion. Extra champagne at Christmas, and here's another step up the management tree. All good. Except for the fact that from about week six in the role I start finding nicely hidden problems under everything I turn over. By the end of January, I had a good handle on the first big issue.

Over about the previous three years, you know there's been a fair bit of publicity about new paramedic road-side interventions in major trauma cases. Everyone's been enthusiastic, including you guys at Queens. Well some joint case reviews have looked at trends over the last two years, and what we're seeing is a high rate of procedural complications on scene, prolonged scene times while procedures are done and probably, though we aren't certain yet, an increased death rate in cases with no transport to hospital. It all smells like paramedics choosing to 'stay and play', as you guys sometimes like to say, rather than getting the patients to hospital where they can get care from a full trauma team. Give them a new toy and you can't get them to put it down.

Well, I'm thinking this is not good, and registered my lack of appreciation with the arsehole that vacated the job and handed me the steaming pile. I thought for a while that he probably hadn't known about all this until I stumbled on the full extent of the shit sandwich in February.

So, we were looking at the early data in our quarterly report on pain relief in trauma patients. We've been auditing this since the changes made across the system three years ago, and particularly since we introduced some new drugs and protocols last year. Blind Freddy could see even in the preliminary data that there had been a major change with really, and I mean majorly, worsening pain control. You know typically we used to see people with significant injuries have their pain score reduced from seven or eight out of ten down to two or three. Now the reductions were down to maybe five or six at best. But the truly bizarre thing was that when we scratched a bit deeper, the performance change was only on the west side. So, we started thinking what are the paramedics on the west side doing different? Are they interpreting the guidelines differently? Have they misinterpreted the new education package and drug protocols, or what?

I got two guys onto it and had them go through the cases very thoroughly. I mean ten-hour days, every case, fine-toothed comb, every detail, for the best part of two weeks, until WTF, the common thread appears. Mastenyl.

Every case where there had been an inferior response to pain killers, the patient had been treated with Mastenyl.'

Harvey shifted in his seat. 'I guess you read that paper from the UK about the paramedics substituting water for Mastenyl in the vials, and keeping the good juice for themselves?'

'It was New Zealand,' replied Rob, 'and, yep, it was one of several reports we managed to dig up. They suppressed some of the reports, and we couldn't find any Australian cases, but we were confident that this would explain our problem.

So here I am sitting on two severely intense issues, both relating to expensive service 'improvements' that politicians have gone to town on and our managers and board have been crowing about everywhere. I'm thinking: no one is going to want to hear these stories and, in my experience, the pain associated with this kind of mayhem is unlikely to be felt at the right level. More likely it will all roll down hill, and it's not beyond the realms of possibilities that the messenger will be shot.'

'Let me get this straight,' Harvey said. 'This all played out in February and it's now the beginning of April. Where was the explosion I missed? I haven't heard a thing about this.'

'That's because there has been nothing to hear, Harvey. I pushed this upstairs with a rocket, expecting to be summoned to the exec third-degree please-explain-session. But zip happened. So I start following up and get some 'advice' from my boss that this is being investigated by a special panel and, 'thanks very much, please keep this confidential, and by the way management have decided to centralise the incident management and standards part of my role so that I won't need to be chairing that committee or doing that role… Oh and by the way 'the guy replacing you has already been briefed, so no handover will be needed'. Thank you and piss off back to your Divisional role asap (and quietly).'

Rob was on a roll now. 'By now I'm thinking this is not a healthy scenario. I've found something, which was probably known about for some time and done the classic new-guy-in-the-job uncovers the murky and severely politically embarrassing truth routine. I'm feeling about as comfortable as an uncommitted terrorist in a suicide vest. Then, happy days, two or three weeks ago, and just by coincidence, one morning as I head off to work, I find a half-blood-filled syringe neatly tucked under the wiper on the car windshield.' Swallowing the last of his coffee, Rob seems to be finished. Harvey pauses, just in case.

'So, there you go, Harvey. That's where we're at. I'm sorry I haven't filled you in earlier, pal. I don't know where this is going but as far as I can see, no one is doing anything. If there was an investigation going on, I would have heard about it, and I'm assuming the board and government haven't been briefed, or this would have leaked for sure. I seriously don't know what to do, but I'm assuming there is risk attached if I open my mouth.'

'Jesus Christ,' Harvey almost whispers. 'This is nasty and has obviously got some dangerous and possibly unhinged folk excited. I can't quite work it out though, Rob – the first part of your story about paramedic trauma care could be 'just one of those things'. You know, policy changed due to what people thought was a promising idea at the time. Turned out to be wrong, so OK, fess up and fix it.

Problem two is the worry, and the fact that it has snowballed and become big enough to be detectable so quickly suggests something organised behind the scenes. More worrying. Either way, are they connected somehow? Is that why you've been shafted? If there is a link, who has what to gain or lose through this? If you're going to do anything more about this, then that's the angle we need to sort out and understand. Your windshield message was blunt. No coincidence. What you found would risk shining a light on some people with a lot to lose, and who also probably have some unpleasant associates.'

Harvey's mind was reeling. 'Looks to me like you've uncovered two shitpiles. The first is big enough to bring down the EMS executive plus or minus government ministers at the next election. The second could do much the same and with a nastier element to it if there's more involved than Mastenyl, or an organised group behind it. Maybe this's more likely than I want to think about – what's happening must be big if we're seeing patient effects at the level you described across a whole area.'

Rob nodded. 'This isn't just one or two guys getting their jollies from some pilfered Mastenyl – more likely it's a small organised group working a system for their own use. The volumes of Mastenyl wouldn't be high enough for them to turn this commercial. My money is on these being reasonably intelligent addicts who obviously have careers and lives to lose. Did the threat come from them or the bigger picture losers? I don't know.'

'That's where I ended up too.' Jess finally got a word in. 'The real question now is what to do or not do about it? That's what we've been dealing with and what's stressing us out. Do we try to take this back up the tree internally? Hard to get enthusiastic about that option, given what happened to Rob's position… Do we go to the cops about the syringe? I can hear it now, "Thanks for the report but one syringe does not equal a death threat or conspiracy"… '

Harvey isn't sure what advice to give, which he decides means it's better to keep quiet, but this is uncomfortably akin to what he's dealing with himself.

Jess and Rob were looking to him for advice, but he was still trying to solve his own problem. Should they just try again and re-table their cases within each organisation and wait for a response? Should they go directly to the health department? Together? Separately? Should they trigger the State whistle-blower legislation and risk their luck with that system protecting them? Should they look for a softer approach?

After an hour, another coffee, lots of backward and forward scenario runs and more than a few 'what if' tests, Harvey still wasn't sure which path to take. Jess and Rob were no wiser, but the three of them agreed they needed a plan. The impromptu think-tank adjourned with a vow to catch up the following weekend. Harvey would talk it through with Alex at work tomorrow; maybe he would have some bright ideas after his couple of days off. It all needed some more thought and hopefully, or at least perhaps – they would get a plan settled next week. Or not.

Harvey left the café with a feeling of gut-twisting concern.

Chapter 10

Week of 1 April 2019

Harvey and Alex were sitting in the insipidly sunlit courtyard beside the hospital café, a place where they were sure of privacy, and had often retreated for those more serious times in a cone of silence.

'Alex, I feel like this is going nowhere. You've been blocked on the notifications and Root Cause Analysis on the diabetic death and they won't entertain an open investigation and report.'

'The real question,' Alex replied 'is why the hesitancy? Why the concern about raising the issue with the Health Department? There must be an explanation that we're missing, and it's not just a stupidity issue. For Queens exec to sit on this means either there's a serious directive from beyond about 'no bad news' or the exec group or individuals have something to lose directly if they follow through on this. I don't get it and I've never seen such a run of obvious cover-ups before. Though with what you've said about the EMS and Rob Massey's position I'm starting to think this is bigger than just Queens. It's quite a coincidence to have a couple of serious hush issues happening at once in distinct parts of the health system. There's got to be more to it.'

Harvey and Alex had been debating options for escalation of their concerns for half an hour and still couldn't agree the best strategy.

The ED was quiet for a Monday morning, so they'd retreated to Alex's office to go over what Harvey had been told by Rob the day before.

'There is a way we could test that theory you know,' said Harvey, 'and maybe this is smarter than dropping a bomb on something that may just be our paranoia playing up. Next week we have our quarterly clinical outcomes round-table at the health department. There'll be governance leaders from all over the city and a lot of data hitting the table… it shouldn't be hard for me to get an agenda item tabled looking at the proportion of incident reviews with recommendations for Root Cause Analysis that have been deferred for in-house review rather than reported to the health department. If there is something going on, this is a group that will catch on fast – there's no shortage of righteous warriors around the table, not to mention the handful that see a major bureaucratic conspiracy sitting behind every decision the department makes.'

'I think you're onto something there, Harvey. The EMS governance guys will be there as well, so it covers off on Rob's issue to a degree. You'll need to get something through to the department admin staff by tomorrow to get this on the agenda. They won't issue the papers and agenda till Wednesday, so you should be fine.'

'OK, I'll draft something this afternoon and flick it to you for a look. In the meantime, though, I'm going to prep a response to the CEO about our case. I know he's given you the word, but Alex, at the end of the day this area falls in my portfolio and I feel that I need to formally respond. I don't agree with the decision he's taken to go with an internal review of the diabetic death and I need to register my opinion. I don't expect I'll even get a response, but at least I'll be able to live with myself and sleep nights. By the way what's happening with the departmental review he hit you with? I've got to say that's one of the most obvious shut-down manoeuvres I've ever seen.'

Alex chuckled. 'Now, why would you be so cynical, Harvey? I don't know what's happening with the review, but no doubt it will realise the result it is tailored to achieve, if it gets going. Isn't that the way these things always go?' He finished with a resigned grin.

Harvey left to write his draft agenda item and wondered to himself how much longer Alex would stick this out. He wasn't well, didn't need to work and must be getting to the end of his tolerance for this level of fucked up game-playing. He restated his vow to himself that he would never take on a management role like Alex.

By midday, Harvey had headed down to the ED. He had a half shift on the floor today and, as always, looked forward to the time he spent there, insulated from administrivia by the woes and suffering of the patients who passed through on the endless healthcare conveyer belt the ED provides.

It was a respectable shift. He was working with a good team that smoothly toiled through the day with friendly humour spending time with the patients and their families then accelerating the pace when the intensity or volume demanded. And then up another notch when the trauma arrived late in the shift. That went smoothly, too, and the young motorcyclist was packed off to the OR for repairs, which was more than could be said for his pillion passenger girlfriend who didn't make it to hospital and had been packed off to the morgue. When he heard that from the local cops who'd come to interview the driver, Harvey's thought about the conversation with Rob and Jess yesterday. A day later, when left to his own thoughts, it was difficult for him to swallow their mutual theories. He started to wonder if there could be any level of collusion behind what Rob had described – all his experience told him incompetence was more likely than conspiracy when it came to things going wrong in this business; and who in their right mind would contrive to play Machiavellian games with the health system, patients' lives, peoples' wellbeing? But then again that man himself had said that 'politics have no relation to morals'…

Harvey put his feet up at home that evening and chilled with a beer and the numbingly repetitive news broadcast on cable. Eventually Stephen King challenged him to escape vegetation in front of the TV and he spent the evening immersed in strangeness – a lot like the last few days in his real world. He rang Rob to update him on the conversation with Alex and the plans for the meeting next week. They agreed to catch up next weekend for more tennis and strategizing.

Tuesday was another civilised shift in the ED and the day went quickly. By 4pm Harvey had finished up and had completed his whiteboard list of to-dos for his admin day tomorrow. The list wasn't long for a change, but the response to the CEO was at the top. He would need to draft it carefully.

Queens was Roger Hutten's first CEO job and he'd only been in the post for 18 months, having impressed his way up the corporate health ladder, aided by a booster rocket from his better half. As important as he felt he was (and projected himself), there was consensus that his partner, Jane Chantier was the prime mover in their household. She was a career executive and aspiring politician, now rising-star Health Department Secretary and with a personality that would make Narcissus feel humble. She had her eyes on a safe seat at the upcoming election and no doubt was aiming for a quick appointment into the Health Ministry. Roger had been an effective CEO so far. He had a reputation for all those 'good CEO' behaviours – delivering the goods, meeting targets and coming in on budget, which was fortunate because anything less would have left him short of his self-opinion. He also had a reputation for extravagant living, which was reflected in his waistline and supported by a pompous nature. His first six months had been the typical slice and dice of the existing hospital leaders followed by a raft of new appointments to guarantee him a loyal and indebted inner circle. Since then the pattern had been less explosive and more a progressive tightening of purse strings and the odd noose. Harvey didn't like him much, having formed an opinion that Hutten was just another marginally-capable, self-interested climber who would be as happy working in the refuse industry as in health… if he felt important enough. Patients were incidental.

―∿∿⊢∿―

Despite his best plans, Harvey started the next day with a welcomed distraction from Elli Clemence, by way of an overnight email.

The production team were happy with the draft script for the 'Truth' podcast. Elli's producer had tracked some edits in the document and Harvey reviewed them, agreeing with the handful of suggestions. They were happy to go with the talk as a straight up piece, without a compere or interviewer. Everyone would hear Harvey's voice in a self-consciously passionate delivery of his beliefs on knowledge and truth – views that would not lend themselves to punctuation with hammy fashioned questions. The producer, however, did think a Q&A approach to the next topic of 'Challenge' would offer a contrasting style and, by the way, could they have a draft of that by next week?! Say goodbye to another Saturday. Loquitur had scheduled release of the Brussels colloquium next weekend, followed by weekly releases of the rest of the podcasts. Harvey was happy he could stay a couple of weeks ahead of the production dates, finding the whole thing a bit of a blast and a welcome diversion from the day-to-day.

—⎦⎣—⎦⎣—

His email response to the CEO hose-down posed more of a challenge and Harvey spent a good part of the morning drafting and redrafting. He needed to restate the argument for external review of the case and for the provision of resources to resolve the issues he knew had led to this disaster. He'd started by assuming that the CEO had reached his position for a specific reason. He tried to imagine what that reason might be and, before long, decided that whatever private theory he constructed about it, his response was unlikely to be effective. He knew Hutten's decision didn't fit with hospital or health department policy. Hutten was usually deliberate – he didn't do things impulsively. However, this wasn't the first executive to decide about 'not applying' policy 'with discretion'. Harvey also knew straight up that any challenge he made would be an irritation and could be seen as a threat. What's more he felt certain Hutten would not change his position, meaning this was a lose-lose situation. Fuck it, he thought, sometimes you just need to play the game knowing you are going to lose.

He chose his words carefully and copied in Alex, having decided not to ask him to review the message before sending it, leaving him a manager's escape based on 'plausible deniability'.

The angle Harvey took in the end was to raise a risk-flavoured flag. He knew that Hutten would understand the messaging and would choose to act or (probably) not. He finished his email with a simple and clear conclusion:

'Regarding the Case of JP, reviewed Monday 25 March 2019: I have been informed by departmental management that it is the hospital's decision not to pursue external Root Cause Analysis or report the case to the Health Department.

I have assumed that active executive consideration has been given to the specific mandatory requirements of the Health Department policy, of the Open Disclosure policy and of the Hospital Insurer's expectation for notification of level one cases.

I remain available to progress any further actions as requested and strongly recommend review of this decision, together with application of normal policy and effective governance standards.

Yours Sincerely, etc.'

Harvey didn't stop to wonder if he would receive a response.

He spent the afternoon working on some teaching material he needed to finalise for the next week and then moved on to patching some roster problems that had appeared over the last few days. Staff scheduling was the only downside to his job, and it was something that Harvey neither enjoyed nor mastered, which meant that from time-to-time, the schedule fell over with no reserves for vacant slots... The extra shift on Sunday had Harvey's name all over it and would consume his tennis arrangements. He reminded himself to let Rob know – hopefully one day on the following weekend would be OK for a game and maybe a lazy lunch with him and Jess to follow.

His in-box pinged. Harvey suspended his early rumination on an extended lunch break ...

From: Jemima Reynolds <J_Reynolds.dhs@healthnsw.org>
Subject: Agenda Quarterly Health Dept Clinical Outcomes
        Roundtable
Date: 3 April 2019 at 15:38:05 AEST
To: Harvey Pearce

Dear Professor Pearce

Thank you for your email of last week and for the suggested agenda item (Reporting rates of Critical Incidents for Root Cause Analysis).

I have raised the matter with the Chair (Todd Fenland, Exec Director Quality and Safety at Queens Hospital) who has let me know today that our agenda for next week is rather full and suggests holding this matter over until later in the year or referring it to the Review Unit directly.

You may wish to follow up with Mr Fenland at your hospital. I am sorry I am unable to progress your request at this time.

Sincerely

Jemima Reynolds

Senior Project Officer, Operational Quality & Safety, DHS, NSW.

Harvey read the email for the third time and sat staring at his screen with no expectation that anything would change on it or that a solution to his unasked question would appear from the dark web. What the hell. He wasn't even sure what question to ask himself. He was about to dial Fenland's number and say what? He wasn't sure. But a knock at the door saved him from an impetuous conversation, which was also probably pointless.

From the look on Andrew's face, Harvey knew that Fenland would have to wait. Andrew Raven was one of the more experienced lead nurses in the ED and having trained and then staffed at Queens for the last twelve years, knew almost everything that was going on. He was smart, had a nose for trouble and was always clued in to any of the staff that may be making hard work of the ED – and there were usually a few. No one ever slipped under Andrew's radar, which was something Harvey couldn't boast, but could envy.

'Hi Andrew, what's up?'

'Hey, Harvey, I just wanted to give you a heads up. You know we are still doing those pointless certifications for the Coroner? You know they still bring the recently dearly departed here – the one's that don't have a doctor present at the death and our docs do the life-extinct certification so they can transport to the morgue.'

'Yeah, Yeah, Nonsensical exercise really, I don't think we've ever seen one that wasn't dead!' quipped Harvey.

'Correct,' replied Andrew. 'But what we did have yesterday was a rebounder. One of the patients we saw on Monday came back 'in the van', which I presume isn't the first time. Problem is that Paul Fritz, who looked after our diabetic disaster the other week, also saw said patient on Monday, a forty-something man with chest pain that was clearly cardiac. Unfortunately, Paul also happened to be the duty resident yesterday who did the van certification. I saw him today and he looks like he hasn't slept for a month. I don't think there was any problem in his management of the case – I know he referred on and that the cardiology team saw the guy, though I don't know what became of him or what the plans were. He was still here Monday night when I went off. Either way I'm thinking young doc Fritz is in the short line for a touch of the PTSD if this keeps happening and either way maybe you'd want to know.'

'Thanks Andy, I'll have a word with him – what's it like out there at the moment?'

'Remarkably under control.' Andrew crossed his fingers and arms simultaneously. 'It's been 'q-u-i-e-t' all shift' he spelled out. No one ever says the q word in the ED for fear of precipitating chaos. 'I'll send Paul to you.'

It was nearly 4 pm and Harvey was keen to get home. All the same this wouldn't take long and was important. The newer staff in the ED were always a bit at risk when it came to fallout from the misery that was quite often a part of their work. Most did fine, but every now and then there was someone who needed a bit of extra support, and occasionally there'd be a nurse or doc who was a total shit-magnet, or so it seemed.

Paul Fritz was in the office in under five minutes and didn't need a lot of explanation from Harvey about the reason for their discussion.

'I'm OK,' said Paul, 'I saw the peer support psychologist and we had a chat – I think I'm coping fine and you don't need to worry about me. The case on Monday was incredibly sad but was clinically straight forward, and I had done my assessment and referred the guy to cardiology after reaching a conclusion that he needed to come into hospital for investigation. It was a first episode 'chest pain assessment' in a 40-year-old and both he and his family were anxious.'

'Why was he sent home?' said Harvey.

'I wasn't there when he was sent home,' Paul said. 'But the next day I heard the admission was deferred because of "no bed available". They loaded him on some start-up meds, for review the following day. I don't know anything else other than that I certified him when he came through in the Coroner's van.' Harvey noticed the faintest crack in Paul's voice, and eyes that betrayed the potential of a tear.

'Andy was right,' said Paul. 'I didn't sleep much last night, but then I figured who would if they were in my shoes? It threw me to see him dead. Something's fucked up about the fact that he wasn't admitted, but I'm fairly happy it's not my fault this time.'

Harvey spent the next fifteen minutes with Paul, clarifying detail and drafting an email to the head of cardiology. The case would be reported for investigation and the Coroner's office would already be involved. It was up to the cardiology department to complete this review and supply the report, but the ED had a stake in it and Harvey was keen to get feedback asap – his staff would need reassurance that a review would be objective, and he would also activate the peer support team.

Harvey copied the email to Alex's in-box with an indiscreet and frustrated subject line: Another death – looks like a bed access/system failure.

Paul went back to his shift and Harvey went home. Both had something extra to think about, and tonight it would be Harvey's turn not to sleep.

Before heading home, where Harvey knew he would spend the evening digesting the activities of an unsatisfying day, he put in a call to Todd Fenland. His phone rang out, so he left a message:

'Hi Todd, Harvey Pearce here. I wanted to talk about the agenda item I had proposed for Monday's meeting – I think it is reasonably important that we get this item up for discussion. Can you please give me a call back on my mobile? Anytime is fine. By the way there has been another fucking death that cardiology will no doubt report to you. Is this one also not going to be investigated?'

The second he hung up he regretted the message. 'Take a breath,' he told himself; 'cut the crap' he replied.

Harvey wasn't surprised to hear nothing from Fenland, though he had thought that by week's end there could've been a prospect of a reply from him or the CEO.

At least the cardiology risk manager had got back to him with a promise of a completed review with feedback by mid next week. Thank God some of us care and can communicate, thought Harvey.

The weekend arrived but did not thrill Harvey. He woke on Saturday and decided a little work-life balance improvement might be in order. Today was reserved for work on 'Challenge' and tomorrow an extra shift covering a schedule gap in the ED. At least next week he could take Friday off to compensate and maybe head out of town.

Chapter 11

Cut the Crap - CHALLENGE

In the previous podcast, I presented some thoughts about Truth and how we use and abuse knowledge. Today I'll discuss another topic, Challenge, and I hope to provide you with another tool and a way of thinking that will help you to cut the crap!

To help me with this podcast, let me introduce Elli Clemence, from our production company Loquitur.

ELLI

Thank you, Professor Pearce. Loquitur is proud and privileged to present this series of podcasts and I just wanted to spend a moment acknowledging the work you have done here. The ideas you're presenting and sharing are clear and packaged in a way that seems to offer a simple strategy that most of us could benefit from applying. Our world has become more and more complicated, artificial and stressful, and I think that your approach is resonating with a lot of people who want to focus on what matters; where possible, to eliminate as much of the confounding mess that we come across in life. Harvey, the idea of doing this in a way that people can relate to, which doesn't have to be part of a movement or religion or fad, but which spins around a mantra we're all familiar with is brilliant!

Your last presentation on Truth raised some provocative ideas but I suspect today you are going to take us to another perplexing place – the idea that challenge can be a core part of making our lives better is certainly something to think about. We see so much confrontation in the world, which is negative between nations, politics, individuals.... What do you mean by challenge?

HARVEY

Thank you for the kind words.

To me, challenge is mainly about the awareness and acknowledgement of what is around us, seeing this with a critical eye, with analysis. It's remarkably easy to look past what's right in front of us and not see what's really going on, not see the opportunity.

So, it is important that we train our minds to be more critical of our world. On a small scale this could be as simple as learning not to accept the status quo and challenging ourselves to do something different. For example, the supermarket checkout. If we continue to use plastic bags to carry our groceries, there is no doubt we will contribute to environmental decline. If we take our own reusable bag, we will not. To make that change we need to challenge ourselves, confront a negative behaviour and 'cut the crap'. What sits at the core of that confrontation is awareness of the bag problem and acknowledgement of the rationale to do something.

The other option that we have, of course, is to be blind to issues or wrongs or opportunities to improve, in which case we will not confront those things. In my mind, the first component to challenge is this seeing, acknowledging, realising a need. This seeing is not as simple as the passive opening of our eyes. It requires an active process of looking. Of course, the idea of seeing is just a metaphor – the same can be said of hearing. We often hear things in a physical sense without really listening to a message or to the meaning of the sounds we process. The principle is the same and, in the end, it's about how we process and think about what we encounter in a more active way to achieve awareness and engagement which opens the door to confrontation.

The second part of confrontation is the initiation of a response to the awareness we've gained. From that response comes the potential for change and improvement. The question then becomes, 'What type of response should we have?'

The answer I believe is simply that we must respond – the type or level of response is much less important than the fact that a response occurs. This means we have seen (or heard) and acknowledged. The type and extent of our response will be a matter of context. At the lowest level, we may respond with a conscious registration to do nothing more at this point and at the highest level we may see immediate verbal or physical action. It all depends on the individual, the circumstance, the nature of any threat or issue, the many many drivers that might exist for change. The worst thing we can do is to have no reaction.

The word 'confront' really means to face or to stand facing towards something. Confrontation brings about the potential for change. Without challenging, that potential doesn't exist and I believe this is a long way from conflict or aggression?

ELLI

I understand what you are saying, Professor – the concept of challenging issues can be seen purely as facing up to them, but don't you think that most people see even this constructive spin on challenge and confrontation as potentially aggressive, even hostile?

HARVEY

I hope not. Yet if it is then perhaps that is part of the crap to cut. If our first reaction to facing an issue is the defence to a perceived threat, hostility or aggression, then don't you think we have a problem? If we can't stomach having our ideas, institutions or constructs challenged, isn't there something wrong with our intellectual security?

If, for example, I was to confront or challenge an incorrect decision made by an executive in my hospital, should that be perceived as an immediate affront or should it be seen as another valid and helpful perspective, worthy of consideration?

The everyday world contains too much hostility and we are primed at a survival level to be wary of that. Our wariness around conflict is in part related to this risk-averse set point that we attach to our perception of hostility. If we allow ourselves to equate confrontation with hostility then how do we receive advice? On the other hand, there is no doubt that poor delivery of new concepts may trigger a feeling of attack or hostility – my concept of confrontation as a tool to help our lives needs to be about the challenge of thought, not a demand for action. The person being confronted needs to be allowed to travel the same intellectual journey as the protagonist, but to achieve this they need to be prepared to think. They need to be prepared to acknowledge and develop awareness. Taking a position that doesn't involve such willingness is just crap!

ELLI

What is stopping us from doing what you're suggesting, Harvey? Why do you think you need to state this so explicitly in your strategy? Why don't we challenge the things we should?

HARVEY

Well, a challenge is always a confrontation of the status quo and for many reasons we are wedded to the status quo. At an extremely basic level, if I have accepted a certain way of doing something for a period – or maybe a lifetime - and I am confronted by a new and better way, some people consider this to be evidence that my past position, which I held with conviction, were wrong or at least suboptimal. For many people this type of challenge creates discomfort because it undermines a self-view.

In our small personal worlds there is a quite common general resistance to change. For many of us it is much easier not to confront or to change things – we enjoy stability, control, the known; we fear adjustment, disruption, and sometimes our ability to cope with or manage a new way. It is argued that these things are part of human nature; however, it is as much a part of human nature to strive forward, to develop and to innovate.

Challenge is often seen or perceived as negative or disrespectful, so before we can effectively confront an issue, we often need to overcome our fear of this type of reaction. Most often these positions (of negativity and disrespect) arise in the insecurities and fears of a person we confront. They aren't inherent to the issue under question but are a part of the reaction of those involved. If we focus on the issue and not on the part of stakeholders, the path may be easier. In football parlance, we play the ball, not the man…

Having said all this, I believe a common reason that people do not challenge is that they are submerged in excessively hierarchical cultures, which are not receptive to critique. This type of culture is quite common and is characterised by power gradients and control mechanisms that keep some people 'in their place' and others in control in positions of status or privilege. Those most wedded to these cultures are invariably those least capable of intellectual agility and dynamism, and those least deserving of the privilege and status they occupy. Confronting these cultures can weaken the resolve of the most ardent challenger!

ELLI

I see. So if people can be less reactive or resistive to challenge and we all live in a perfect world where power is set aside and we are all valued equally, then there will be no problem! Confronting issues won't be antagonistic. Harvey, do you really think this advocacy for confrontation is a practical solution? Will it or can it work in the real world?

HARVEY

Will it work?

Yes of course it will work! It's the way every change has ever occurred in the world up to now. To change something, we must always challenge the past and an earlier way of doing something.

Can cultural factors suppress confrontation?

Yes, to some degree a culture not receptive to change is self-reinforcing and will resist confrontation. This is usually through active regulation and processes – the rules, if you like, and the messages we receive to 'toe the line'.

If the knowledge presented is not acted on objectively or in good faith, challenge may be actively resisted. For this to happen, the individual or system being confronted takes an active and conscious position to dismiss the protagonist and their ideas out of hand despite knowing that the challenge is valid and positive. This is different to what happens in a cultural resistance, that is an unthinking, embedded resistance. This active type of resistance is more sinister and goes to the abuse of knowledge and a rejection of truth. This will block confrontation and a drive for change and improvement temporarily; however, this type of position is unsustainable due to the transparency of its injustice. In time it will fall over.

From time to time we come across episodes like this – for example, a scenario where a serious incident occurs in a hospital and a staff member makes a report that should lead to investigation and then rectification of a fault. If the health service were to suppress an investigation for some reason, more individuals may be harmed – both patients and clinical staff. These scenarios are always confronted eventually – it is inevitable. So why resist this confrontation in the first place?

The answer is: a risk of loss to the service, which misguided individuals see as the greater risk – loss of reputation, power, respect, authority, promotion... or some other perversity.

There is, of course, a risk that the confronting protagonist becomes weary. In response to the difficulty of confrontation, we may disguise honest opinion with political correctness or other tools, using words that skate around direct communication, because that may be easier to swallow by those who must be confronted, and which panders itself to ignorance.

Finally, if we are initially unsuccessful in having change follow challenge, we can find ourselves exasperated and worn down by the effort. We may be intimidated; be afraid of the consequences of being a change agent. As a result, sometimes we find ourselves lacking motivation and moved to the space of evasive and avoidance behaviour, where we may dodge an issue altogether rather than risk another unsuccessful confrontation. Fortunately, we can and do naturally learn not to suffer permanent incapacitation through failure or setback.

We are by nature resilient and it is the normal state of humans to use their intellect to progress – not just in little day-to-day things but on the grand stage of humanity. This means confrontation is necessary. We should not fear this quite normal and indispensable part of our existence.

It's simple: you need to challenge the crap before you can cut the crap!

ELLI

Professor Pearce, thank you again for talking through this idea of challenge and the way that it fits into your strategy. I suspect this will help people approach thinking about potential change. I bet it'll also help them communicate as both change proponents and those being challenged by innovative ideas and change proposals. We'll look forward to tuning into your next podcast in a week's time when I believe you will be discussing 'Sufficiency'.

This is Elli Clemence for Loquitur Productions.

Once more, it had taken Harvey almost the whole day to work through his ideas and script out the podcast and he was drained. But again, there was a level of satisfaction that came with the completed task. He attached the document to an email to Elli with the subject line: 'Challenge – there you go!' and retreated to a glass of Pinot from Mount Gisborne. There was an extra shift to deal with tomorrow and he needed to reset.

Chapter 12

Sunday 7 April 2019

By the end of his shift on Sunday, Harvey was ready to erupt.

Ruth Verner was the cardiologist on shift for the ED. Also the clinical director for the service, she was an old friend and had sought out Harvey mid-morning. They retreated to a corner of the staff lounge for coffee and privacy.

'Harvey, I know you contacted our risk manager late last week about the 'community death' case last Tuesday. I just thought I should do the right thing and give you some feedback on this. We had already started to look at this case and it is tragic. The guy was 40, two small kids, with an excellent job and big life. This was his first presentation with chest pain, but he had obvious risk factors and the story was good. It's a no brainer, Harvey, this guy should have been admitted for work up.'

Harvey shifted in his seat and looked over at Ruth. She wasn't just giving him some feedback. Her face told the story of her own discomfort with this case. Ruth was debriefing and sharing the load and Harvey was sure he was about to hear a terrible truth about the preventable loss of a young life.

'Harvey, we had beds available – I mean physical beds. In fact two and we could staff them. Our divisional executive closed the beds as part of a budget-constraint strategy they implemented last week. Admin met with our management team and made it abundantly clear that this was not negotiable, and that more cuts would follow next month. So, we cancelled some nursing shifts and closed the beds. When this guy presented a couple of days later, we were stuffed full. There was no one to discharge that night and no beds in the system or at Emmanuel Hospital either. We thought we could do something by midday the following day, so we sent him home with some meds and arranged a review first thing the next day.' Ruth almost smiled, more of a nervous twitch, really.

'Harvey, I was the consultant last week, I saw him in the ED. I was the one who explained the plan to him and his wife. He wasn't unstable or anything and his pain had completely settled – five years ago we probably wouldn't have even thought about admitting him but, you know how much practice has changed in that space… after the reports in the BMJ last year, everyone's admitting these intermediate risk patients now. I guess the rationale is obvious. What's worse though was that I was short with the couple. I was in a rush, because we had a pile of new cases to see, and I had to wait because his wife was out in the parents' room breast feeding her 9-month-old baby.' Ruth whispered now, almost to herself as she let her own distress and sadness escape.

'I hate that I knew what needed to happen for that guy, and I knew we were denying him care he needed purely on budgeting grounds. We all knew what was best for him; we all knew it was so wrong. Yet we slammed the door in the face of his family.'

Harvey reached across and placed a hand on her forearm. 'Ruth this is awful, and it's not part of the job we signed up for. But you did everything you could for him. You can't create a bed if there isn't one and our resources will always be limited.' He almost believed his own deliberately reassuring mistruths… He continued. 'I guess the positives from this will come from the review of the case and the Coroner's investigation and findings.'

'I'm not convinced, Harvey,' Ruth said. 'I've been told by our Q&S manager that Fenland wants the case reviewed internally, and that we aren't 'required' to complete a departmental review.'

Harvey took a breath and sat quietly, looking down at his shoes. Two cases in as many weeks with unexpected deaths. The usual process: departmental review, referral for Root Cause Analysis, report to Coroner, report to health department. Both cases now have review processes railroaded with referral to internal reviewers in Fenland's department.

This was unbelievable.

Harvey gave Ruth an abridged version of the 'redirection' of the DKA death review and his current concerns about the EMS.

'Ruth, I'm not sure what we can do just yet, but I think we need to check this out. This can't be coincidence. Launching into conspiracy theories isn't healthy, but I'm almost certain I'm not paranoid and if you look at these cases here and the EMS cover up going on at the moment, you really need to start thinking there could be a bigger agenda at work, which is derailing normal case review systems and some of our statutory reporting.'

Ruth threw Harvey a slightly querulous look and said, 'I'm not quite sure what you mean – I know most of our managers are self-interested career-climbers and trust them about as little as you do, but if this is engineered, then we're dealing with something much bigger than a bit of budget buffing or sanitising the annual performance reports. If this is organised or systematic then it's corruption at an extremely high level and across the system – this isn't just some ambitious CEO avoiding a bad report card.'

'That's exactly what I mean,' Harvey said. 'It's like the game has been reset and the approach to any unwelcome news has become 'sit on it'. I mean, there have always been issues where the health system has been short of perfect, but the approach to this stuff had been going in the other direction for nearly a decade. Open disclosure to families, public reporting, use of external reviewers to keep us honest – this stuff has been on track for a long time.

I know not everyone has been happy with the 'open' approach and that some in our noble profession have felt threatened. But, really, I think we all agree it's done a lot to drive transparency and make us all feel a bit more accountable. Lots of good has come out of it and even a fair amount of resource. When the review process is so public it's impossible for anyone to dodge the need to respond with a solution, and, in that way, the necessary fixes become obvious and uncontentious.'

'I don't know, Harvey.' Ruth shifted in her seat. 'I've been here for nearly eight years, and had six years at State before this, and I've seen tight budget situations and admission access problems before. That all kind-of goes with the public health system space, but I've never seen cover up of investigations like this. Seems so bloody obvious that's what's going on. I can fathom it at a one hospital level, but, Harvey, if this is happening here and in the EMS, and those things are connected then there is something very wrong.'

Harvey told Ruth about his failed attempt to get an item on the agenda at the Quarterly Health Department Clinical Outcomes Roundtable meeting scheduled for the next day, and about Fenland's non-response. He needed to think this through before tomorrow and he also needed to get back to the ED floor now. He had no doubt things would be getting busier out there, so he and Ruth finished up with a vow to catch up for coffee later in the week. Harvey liked Ruth; she was a good thinker and they connected easily. She'd be reliable if all this went pear-shaped.

Harvey headed back down the main corridor to the ED and planned to chat with each of the residents to get a feel for the department, and make sure they were all organised and on the right track. His good intentions were side tracked when he heard a scream coming from the resusc bay.

He didn't need to go in to know what awaited him. The familiar nauseating smell of burnt hair and flesh was obvious from outside the curtains surrounding the patient. Harvey entered and looked quickly over the 12-year-old girl lying mostly naked on the bed with obvious burns to her right arm and chest that extended up to the right side of her head.

Her hair looked like one of those bad-taste buzz cuts on that side, but the curled melted hair-ends explained the truth. Her clothing offcuts were charred, and she held her right arm up, staring at her blistering red hand.

He went over to the resident and the two paramedics talking in the corner to learn that this was another story of barbeque-lighting gone wrong, with a bottle of accelerant spilling and exploding and scorching the right side of a kid who shouldn't have been anywhere near it. Harvey heard a story like this a couple of times per year and along with the predictable 'injury-of-sixty-year-old-male-falling-from-ladder', was one of the big preventable injuries that he kept raising with the public health injury prevention unit.

But the issue in the ED now wasn't injury prevention it was about getting this girl's pain controlled and the burns cleaned and dressed before they could be assessed by the Burn Unit.

'How much analgesia has she had?' asked Harvey.

The paramedic checked his running sheet and turned back to Harvey. 'She's had nearly 150 mics of Mastenyl, Professor Pearce; that's a bit over 2.5 mics per kg. We've maxed out our protocol on the dose, so had to get her in here asap.'

Harvey turned to the resident and asked to get a Mastenyl infusion going and to arrange some Ketamine for the girl.

'But won't we be exceeding recommended doses with that?' asked the resident.

Harvey turned back to the three of them with a face not to be argued with. 'No, Josh, the dose will be OK. BTW, I want the EMS Mastenyl vial and discard syringe now. I want them bagged and sealed. I know you guys told me she has received 150 of Mastenyl, but she doesn't look like that to me. I'm sure you've given her a correctly calculated dose of whatever was in that vial, but I'm betting this girl has had extraordinarily little opiate.'

'What are you saying, Professor Pearce?' The more senior paramedic flinched.

'I'm saying that I want the large security officer outside this cubicle to go with you to the ambulance and for you to hand him the items I just asked you for, after which he'll bag them. When we've sorted this girl, I'll arrange for them to go to the lab for analysis.'

'Are you suggesting we've got her dose or the infusion wrong?' asked the other paramedic.

'No,' replied Harvey, 'but given what I've heard lately and the degree of pain this girl has, after what sounds to be a thoroughly adequate dose of analgesic, I think we need to at least check the vial that you've used today to make sure there is no issue with it.'

Harvey walked over to the girl. The resident ordered the drugs he had specified and within 5 minutes she had started to settle. There was no way this girl had received 150 mics of Mastenyl, and Harvey knew it. He checked the paramedic's IV line. It seemed fine. Clearly, she'd received the IV fluids and the drugs the paramedic had administered, whatever they were.

The security officer returned with the Mastenyl vial and discard syringe, which the paramedic signed over to Harvey. He bagged and secured the items. The department was under control, so Harvey took the items to the Tox lab himself and handed them to the tech. The assay was quick to perform and he'd have an answer inside half an hour, so Harvey headed for a coffee. The calculation was simple – the Mastenyl vial should contain a concentration of 50 mic/ml, and the syringe diluted for the IV push should contain around 10 mic/ml, allowing for some small dilution error. Standard concentrations for every patient.

Twenty minutes later, Harvey took the call from the Tox tech.

'Hey Professor Pearce, you've got a problem there,' started the tech. 'First up, the vial concentration is 12.01 mic/ml and the syringe is 2.35 mic/ml. So what you have is a vial with a drug concentration eighty per cent lower than it should be. The syringe concentration is about right if these paramedics had drawn up the Mastenyl from this ampoule and applied the dilution they're meant to under protocol. Second up: the vial has been tampered with – there's a small puncture in the side seal on the cap. My bet is that the vial has been milked, and eighty per cent of the Mastenyl has been replaced with water or saline.'

Harvey's suspicion, which he had Rob Massey to thank for, was right. Where had the Mastenyl gone? Harvey figured it was almost impossible these paramedics would have deliberately short-changed a 12-year-old girl screaming in pain, so the drug tampering must have happened upstream somewhere.

The production line? Unlikely. Security in the factories would be huge and Harvey assumed they would have CCTV and security everywhere. The transport and distribution company? Same story, unlikely but a possibility. The EMS was the most likely theft point, with several possibilities. The vial would have been in storage, would've been delivered to a base, would've been handled by other paramedics using the drug kit on earlier shifts. There was no way for

Harvey to know or work out exactly what had happened in this case, but he knew Rob probably had the answer.

Harvey was back in the ED when the paramedics were getting ready to leave. He went over to them and straight up lied, telling them he'd have a formal report from the lab tomorrow but that they should report the case in the meantime. Apparently, they'd already rung their controller and supervisor. Having a hospital test an EMS narcotic vial was no every-day event. By Monday morning, this would be a big deal …

The EMS 'bat-phone' blared at the main ED desk. Harvey had five minutes for a quick pee break before a sick asthmatic arrived post-arrest. Paul Fritz was the senior resident on duty, so Harvey allocated the case to him and hovered in the background supervising. He was confident about Paul's ability, but wanted to see him in action after the recent cases.

As it was, Paul handled the case well. The patient was properly sick, on a ventilator and with several infusions running. Paul coordinated his team well and between him and the nurses and techs, the patient was ready for ICU transfer inside an hour. Before the transfer, Paul came over to Harvey to run through the case summary – the customary checkpoint with the duty consultant – before the patient went to the CT scanner on his way up to ICU.

'Prof Pearce,' began Paul, applying the familiar version of Harvey's formal title, 'I'm happy with Mr Barty now, but I am planning a scan for him on the way upstairs. He's a 28-year-old with a high-risk flag for anaphylaxis and allergy presentations and has come in from Hyde Park in the city where he collapsed about 2.15pm. Known asthmatic, he had preventers with him and info from bystanders says he was using them. The EMS were there fast and got ICU paramedic backup within a couple of minutes. It looks like he lost consciousness ten minutes or so after they were on scene, and then got intubated. It looks like the tube was difficult and needed multiple attempts, but it was eventually secured, infusions started, and he was transported. He lost cardiac output for a while with a bradycardic arrest and got 15 minutes of CPR and a pile of adrenaline. We've settled him on the ventilator and started an adrenaline infusion but, so far, he hasn't needed any sedation – he's not doing much…. I'm worried he's had significant down time and maybe a hypoxic brain injury.'

'Hold on, Paul,' Harvey said, 'did you say he came in from Hyde Park?'

'Correct, Prof.'

'Are you sure about the times, Paul? It's nearly 4.30pm now and he's been here a bit over an hour?'

Fritz checked the times on his ED record and the running sheet and turned back to Harvey. 'Yes, they're correct. Call was 2.15pm, EMS on scene at 2.19pm, second crew at 2.23pm, then they departed the scene at 3.11pm. Arrived here 3.16pm.'

Oh crap, thought Harvey, six minutes from hospital, and the paramedics have spent nearly an hour at the scene. An intubation they couldn't manage, an arrest they probably caused, and all in the back of a truck when we were here waiting, just minutes away, with all our resources and a team of specialists… to at least give this guy a chance…

Chapter 13

Week of 8 April 2019

Monday arrived and Harvey rose feeling unrested and irritated. He had slept poorly and, after waking at three, the rest of the night was spent tossing and turning with the events of recent days interrupting every attempt to. He got up before the sun, made a coffee and picked up the local news channel on his iPad. First up: the northern beach area of Gosford is preparing for the local marathon next month. This was not Harvey's idea of fun. He wondered how many would keel over this year.

The weather: foul for the next three days with misty rain and overcast skies. Then: Health Secretary Chantier announces a building and infrastructure refresh to total $450 million. Of course, just in time for the election.

Resting his head back in his chair, he allowed his eyes to close. Even a couple of hours of relaxed sleep, punctuated by nothingness, with a refreshed alive wakeup would be nice. Maybe someone else in the house to share some thoughts with in the middle of the night would be nice. Having a life – now that would be nice. He couldn't settle and within a few minutes his brain was back to a dead diabetic, the discharged cardiac patient, the kid with no pain relief, Rob's story of the EMS. Harvey was not great at turning off and a night like this wasn't new to him. He was the sort who wouldn't let his mind settle till he had a plan or at least reached a conclusion. It was a curse but he enjoyed his thoughts at the same time, happy when creativity appeared or a plan blossomed. Now, though, he had a head full of knotted questions.

The only answer was to get out of bed and do something. Doing something, anything, occupied his brain and demanded concentration on a task, something tangible, something real. Anything was better than the circular ruminations about thoughts inflated by the darkness. Contorted thoughts, assuming more importance than they deserved, could sometimes invade a fatigued mind as it tried to force its way into sleep. It was better to be out of bed and doing something, even something banal that didn't need doing anytime soon.

Over the morning a plan took shape for Harvey. A run through a cool, autumn-toned botanical gardens, another coffee, and his home-made version of eggs and smashed avo (which he found both comforting and disturbingly millennial), all helped to clear and settle his thoughts. He needed to follow up on the case from yesterday and contact Rob after the regional clinical outcomes meeting today. At the meeting, he would see Jemima Reynolds from Health and quietly probe about recent reporting rates and incident management across the state. Fenland may also be up for a chat, if Harvey nailed his foot to the floor. Small steps.

The meeting was in Room 23.19 in the Health Department building on Christie Street. Harvey arrived fifteen minutes early and, as expected, Jemima was in the meeting room preparing the room and chairing papers for Fenland.

'Good afternoon, Harvey, coffee's in the usual place.' Jemima knew Harvey well as a regular attendee of Health Department meetings over several years. He was known by Departmental staff as a straight shooter, sometimes blunt in delivery, but objective and fair. Unlike the chair and most of the hospital managers around, Jemima enjoyed working with Harvey who was not a 'game-player'.

'What's news, Jemima?' Harvey made his way to the coffee trolley, hoping he may also find a chocolate biscuit to assuage his sleep-deprived fatigue.

'Oh, not much, Harvey, just half a billion health dollars in funding just popped up – don't you read the newspaper? I think that'll keep us busy in here for the next five years!'

'Yes, I did see that this morning and assumed it was electioneering. Wasn't it all about infrastructure?'

'Uh ha, and BTW congratulations – Queens is getting just over $150 million of it for a refresh of the south wing and to build a new community treatment centre.'

Harvey thought for a moment. 'But that's whacky, the south wing is dated but not too bad, and I thought we'd negotiated to share the Harbourside Community Centre. It's only a couple of years old and has heaps of capacity.'

'Between you and me,' replied Jemima, 'A lot of eyebrows have gone up in here. No one seems to know exactly which bag the premier has pulled this money out of and the department had been lobbying hard for more staffing and service-delivery dollars, not for building works. Lots of pre-election thinking seems to be going on …'

Harvey stopped for a moment. 'Hmm, is that also why we seem to be focussing on good news stories and hosing down the tricky conversations and root cause analyses? That wouldn't have anything to do with why my agenda item didn't get added for today would it?'

'Now, Harvey it would be wrong to compromise my role as a government employee and either confirm or deny such a scandalous speculation.' Jemima pouted. After her half-joke, she looked sad for a moment and turned her back. 'This stuff is what vexes me about this job – who stands to gain the most out of half a billion in building announced four months before the polls?'

Turning back to him she said, 'Oh, and hot gossip, Harvey. I believe there is an email heading in your direction. The Health Secretary was on the phone to my boss about your podcasts. Aren't you the quiet celebrity! I haven't heard them, but a couple of people around here have mentioned them – they seem to be getting a good reception.'

Harvey blushed just a little, silently annoying himself. 'That must be another Harvey Pearce. To be honest, you're the first person who's said anything to me about them. I suspect they're going to stir the pot a little but hey … '

Todd Fenland entered the room, dressed in his relentless blazer and wearing a face of preoccupation. 'Afternoon, Jemima, Harvey. Jemima can I just go through a couple of items on the agenda with you? And Harvey have you got five minutes after the meeting?'

'Sure,' they replied in coincidental unison. The room started to fill.

About ninety minutes later, the meeting wrapped up, after covering the ridiculously full agenda. Harvey thought he had never been to a meeting with so much data and so little information – slide after slide of results and reports with no analysis or interpretation to speak of. No discussion of the whys or wherefores. What crap! Outcome data from each of the hospitals was presented but reports from the EMS were held over due to 'administrative issues' in getting them finalised and approved for tabling. The last 30 minutes was spent on a departmental presentation of the strategic planning preparations for next year – rivetingly inconsequential and procrastinating.

Fenland ran the meeting tightly, keeping the diverse group on track, and Harvey had no real opportunity to start a conversation on Root Cause Analysis reporting and investigation trends until the meeting reached 'other business' in the last five minutes. Interestingly, Joe Crompton from The Repat Hospital waded in after Harvey's introduction to the topic, sharing Harvey's questioning of recent processes and reviews. Harvey wondered what lay behind that concern? But Fenland cast him his 'not now' look and shut the discussion down, advising that the item could be put on the agenda for the next meeting in three months.

Harvey knew that to further challenge Fenland at this meeting was pointless. He'd say something like, 'Let's take that on notice and get the department to do some work on the issue for the next meeting'. Then he'd follow up with an awkward conversation back at Queens. At this stage Harvey wasn't certain what he was dealing with so let it go, wondering what Fenland wanted to discuss with him after the meeting, and making a mental note to follow up with Joe Crompton.

―⋀⋀―⋀⋀―

Afterwards, Harvey sat with Fenland in the meeting room, organising themselves at one corner of the boardroom-style table. Fenland began.

'Harvey thanks for staying round – there are a couple of things I wanted to chat to you about. That case review that you sent up to Roger Hutten and me last month was a bit problematic. I know you'll have been looking for a response, and I get from today that you have some concerns about incident reviews at the moment, but really, Harvey, I think you need to allow the system to work through these things. These are complicated reviews and take a little time.

Our quality unit has a whole team to do this work. I don't think it's helpful to be insinuating that there is a problem or that anyone is covering anything up.'

'I'm sorry Todd, but that's not really my concern – what worries me is that we have a standard way of investigating these cases and we –'

'Harvey, no one is suggesting that these investigations not occur, or the cases not be reported in the usual way, but we have taken a view they will be reported and managed through to the department, as required, and after a more thorough investigation at Queens first.'

'What cases?' Harvey's mind was lurching. 'I thought we were talking about the diabetic case – singular – that I sent up to you.'

Todd Fenland wasn't the brightest bulb on the executive Christmas tree and didn't quite have the self-control to hide his displeasure with Harvey's tack.

'Harvey, there are times when an organisation needs to set direction and make decisions about its processes and management, and there will be times that we as individuals are not completely happy with those decisions. The test of a manager and leader is to know when to let an issue run its course, when to let others do their jobs and when not to make unnecessary and distracting noise. To be honest, this kind of behaviour, coming from Alex Bonito and you is exactly why we have initiated the review of the ED. You guys need to learn to play as part of a team and to support management more.'

Play as part of a team or line up with the other sheep, Harvey thought. 'OK Todd, I hear you, and the message is clear, but I just need to let you know that I have a concern. There are cases plural, as you said. We have the diabetic guy; there is the cardiology case from last week; it sounds like there's something happening at Repat from what Joe Crompton said in the meeting; and I believe there are also issues with the EMS right now involving clinical processes, patient outcomes and narcotic abuse. All the ED's in town are choked full of patients who can't get access to beds, and care is suffering. This stuff seems to be building up and we choose not to investigate or follow the normal escalation processes. I don't get it and I don't see why there is a push to bury these questions.'

'Harvey, I think I made our position clear. Your role at Queens includes reporting issues in the standard way and it's the responsibility of my department to further coordinate investigation on behalf of the executive and the hospital. Conflating these issues is simply provocative grandstanding and we don't need or tolerate that kind of behaviour from our clinician leaders. Do I need to explain this any more clearly?' Fenland just couldn't stop himself from adding,

'Harvey, your position as an agitator is quite clear to us, but you need to stop stirring the pot just for the sake of it. A word of advice – let it go, this isn't the right time for a crusade.'

Fenland's advice flabbergasted Harvey. So now advocating for best patient outcomes in the normal way and standing up for systems processes that were geared at improvement makes you an 'agitator'. The best recommendation he could offer was to pull your head in unless you wanted to lose it. Was Fenland just making noise or was there really an 'us' who was upset about his 'agitating'? Who was the us? Fenland and Hutten? Others?

'This is bullshit,' Harvey muttered under his breath.

'You said what?' retorted Fenland. 'If you think you can now be insubordinate as well, I think you'll find yourself in that shit faster than you realised possible.'

Harvey stopped himself, deciding it was time to study the pen he had in front of him, and which he had been using to make notes of the discussion. He spun it on the table, round and round, a habit he found comfortingly distracting in a tense moment and one that irritated Fenland no end. It was clear this conversation was going in the wrong direction, so he retreated.

'I get it,' Harvey said with a level of apparent sincerity that Fenland might just swallow. 'How about I just wait for your response to my report and for the committee to run its investigation then we take it from there?'

Fenland said, 'I think that would be smart, Harvey.' He started packing up his bag but stopped, turning back. 'One other thing – Roger Hutten has asked me to have a word to you about your podcasts. Some in high offices have noticed them, and concerns have been raised about their tone. There is a possibility, don't you think, that people will see them as critical of our system and organisation. Maybe you want to look at trying to be a bit more positive about the world?'

Harvey was about to explode, but somehow checked himself.

'Well, thank you for noticing them but I don't quite get the level of sensitivity. And quite frankly I don't really see that what I do or say in private or academic spaces outside our hospital has anything much to do with you or Mr Hutten. To be honest I think your comments border on institutional paranoia. I'm sorry, Todd, but I need to get back to Queens – I'm on shift in half an hour, so maybe we can continue this another time.'

Harvey didn't wait for a response or stop to think about Fenland's postulation until after he had left the room. Institutional paranoia isn't a real thing. Anxiety has its beginnings in real individuals who feel threatened. But by what exactly? Was it the podcasts? Was it the cases he was pursuing? Harvey was under no illusion that he was in the spotlight but wasn't quite sure of why the intensity was so acute.

―⋀⋁⋀―⋁⋀―

As he finished up at Queens that evening and packed up his iPad and gear. Harvey remembered he owed Rob a call and decided to ring him from home where he could be less guarded about what he said. He still wasn't sure about what to think of Fenland's position today and wasn't comfortable to share all the detail of that conversation with Rob just yet. Maybe he would save that for the weekend when they could sit down properly and chew the fat; maybe he would just keep it to himself. Either way he needed to think this through and needed some time.

'G'day Rob, how are you?'

'Not too bad, Harvey. How did the roundtable go today? Did you get anything useful?'

'I didn't get far,' Harvey replied. 'Just a hint from the department that good news is the strong preference of the department and government right now and that they're pretty obviously pumping sweetener money into the system pre-election. When I asked about root cause analysis processes, Joe Crompton from Repat seemed to get interested. There's definitely something going on at a system level. The vibe from the chair was a deliberate dampener on the whole conversation.' Harvey didn't elaborate on the unsubtle advice he'd received from Fenland.

'I don't get why the department would squash normal processes and investigation of high-risk cases just to avoid a risk of bad press. Presumably this is also because of the election, but this level of sensitivity is seriously odd.'

'Yeah,' Harvey said, 'they seemed happy to waste half the meeting talking about strategic planning and building funding, but the root cause analyses got no oxygen at all. Anyway, leave it with me and I'll see what happens this week. At the current rate, anything could transpire.'

'What do you mean?' asked Rob.

'Oh, just that every day seems to deliver another twist these days. Speaking of which, I had the shift from hell yesterday, which your guys contributed to. I experienced one of your Mastenyl specials and had another EMS case that was a true debacle.'

Harvey gave Rob the abridged version of the two cases from Sunday. They had a predictable impact. Both cases came from east side, Rob's district, so if the reports were processed correctly, they would hit his desk soon. Harvey had just finished writing them up and had sent them by email to the EMS quality-reporting department. Rob assumed the crew with the Mastenyl incident would have logged something already and was equally sure that the crews with the long pre-hospital time and difficult intubation would not have.

'Harv, this sounds like more of the same. Now you know what I'm talking about. If you start looking hard, I guarantee you're going to find more of these cases. Scuttlebutt has it that the Mastenyl issue is widespread, and if you go back to your trauma case audits, the scene management stuff is going to hit you. Nothing has progressed here as far as I know – it all seems to be going under the rug. To be honest I've almost had it.

I also heard from a guy in the UK last week, who said they are sitting on some in-depth research around the whole scene time and EMS treatment interventions area but are having some trouble getting it published. It sounds like they're questioning the place of a lot of the pre-hospital treatments that have become kind-of core paramedic practice.

Harvey, I'll check it out, escalate your report to the executive, and get you some feedback by Friday, OK?

'Thanks mate,' he replied. 'How's Jess?'

'She's doing OK,' Rob said. 'I need to keep our lives under control though. She doesn't need more stress.'

Harvey was already looking forward to the end of the week. Three straight days off was a bit of a luxury, even if Sunday was tagged for his next podcast. The idea of talking into a microphone to that anonymous audience of who knows how many couldn't have thrilled him less this week. Still he would plough on and would give it his best because that was his nature. Sometimes he hated the idea of having to live up to his 'nature' like some self-imposed set of not negotiable standards. But surviving the next few days without imploding was the immediate challenge.

He did well till Wednesday.

Paul Fritz provided Harvey with the news that the asthmatic patient from Sunday had died in ICU overnight. He was twenty-eight, and his family had consented to organ donation, so the upside was a great benefit to ten other patients waiting for various spare parts. He had never regained consciousness and was pronounced brain dead late the day before. Harvey had no doubt this was the result of his cardiac arrest while being 'managed' by the paramedics. That in itself was not an uncommon occurrence – death is part and parcel of the business of ambulance services.

What concerned Harvey was the sequence of events, the proximity of the hospital and the wasting of precious minutes. Why delay at the side of the road when expert help is so close?

Harvey assumed the ICU staff had reported the case and that the Coroner's office would start the appropriate investigation. Given the recent events though, he thought a quick phone call to an acquaintance there could both confirm the report and give him a chance to follow up on the cardiology sent-home-to-die case from last week. At least an interim report should be available on that one.

'Hello Phil, this is Harvey Pearce at Queens, how are you?'

'Travelling well, thanks Harvey. What can I do for you – don't tell me, someone died?'

'Funny Phil, but you used that line last time I called. I was hoping you could just run a check on a report from us from last night or this morning, and I also wanted to follow up on a case from last week.'

'Sure,' he replied.

Phil Vancleef was a long-standing work-buddy of Harvey's who'd arrived from South Africa ten years ago. Harvey had helped him out in a job when he was new to Australian systems, and Phil had stayed in touch over the years, grateful to a mentor. 'As long as you're not going to ask me to do anything illegal. Immoral I can cope with, but illegal worries me a little.'

'Nothing that exciting,' said Harvey. 'The case from overnight was a 28-year-old, Joseph Barty, asthma, brain death, organ donation. I just want to know whether the reporting consultant in our ICU was explicit about the circumstances of the pre-hospital arrest and EMS management.'

'Yeah I know the case. He came in this morning. Incredibly sad this one. Let me just get the document scans up and I'll tell you what we've got... OK, here it is. Let me see. We have the ICU summary – starts with 'Arrested in Hyde Park in the CBD, ambulance response, prolonged pre-hospital time'... Oh, and I see we have the EMS notes and full ED notes scanned as well – absolutely complete for a change. What were you worried about Harvey?'

'Phil, I've been told recently there have been issues with pre-hospital times blowing out and some irregularities in paramedic practice then this case came out of the blue last week. I don't want to prejudice your assessment, but there was an awfully long delay to transport this guy, and apparently a failed procedure – the worry is that this contributed to his death and that there may be a recurring system-level issue behind it.'

'Hmm, OK,' replied Phil. 'I'm not doing this investigation, but I'll pass on the concern diplomatically and make sure it gets a thorough review. What was the other case you wanted to know about?'

'A 40-year-old male, 2 April, died at home after presentation to us the day before with chest pain. Name of Soares, Albert, I think. I was after your post-mortem assessment and will put my money on a myocardial infarction.'

'OK, let me check... Here we are: yes, 2 April, 5.45pm, Surname Soarez. He's listed here as AMI – aren't you clever. No PM or investigation.'

'Hold on, how can that happen?' asked Harvey

'Well, in this case, he was seen by his GP on the morning of 2 April, and his record notes the hospital presentation the day prior. GP's done an ECG, which was diagnostic – AMI, after which the guy arrested and wasn't able to be resuscitated. We did the usual check with the hospital governance team regarding the death within twenty-four hours of hospital discharge. The report from them says, let me see... "assessed in ED, reviewed by consultant, discharged after stable observation for follow up 3 April" ... so on that basis there's nothing for us to do in terms of investigation.'

Harvey straightened in his chair. His hand gripped the handset as he replied: 'What if the notes had said... "unstable angina and acute coronary syndrome in young male, requires admission to hospital for urgent angiogram and observation, no beds available due to budget squeeze, discharged after a brief prayer and crossing of fingers". Would that truth make a difference to the Coroner?'

'Ah yes, just a little,' Phil said, batting back the sarcasm. 'Can you leave this one with me Harvey? I'm going to take this up the tree – I guess the facts in the hospital report are accurate – it's just that some important facts are missing. You know, it may get out that you provided us with cause to reopen an investigation – are you OK with that?'

'Sure,' replied Harvey. 'In fact I'll give them a heads up myself.'

'No problem – maybe about time for us to catch up for some pasta and red?' said Phil.

'Sounds excellent. Talk soon.' Harvey rang off then sighed.

Chapter 14

Friday 12 April 2019

Harvey woke at six, still in his favourite arm chair, accompanied by an empty glass and an almost empty bottle of Chivas. His head hurt nearly as much as his back and his right hand didn't function where he had been resting on it. For a moment he thought he must have had a stroke, until he shook out his hand and noticed the bottle. Greeted by a wave of nausea, he got up and gingerly made his way to the kitchen to prepare a cocktail of ranitidine, paracetamol and lots of water. He needed to sit back down for half an hour to let that kick in.

Friday was to have been my nice restful extra day off, thought Harvey. Instead he was nursing a monster hangover and had already started to reconnect to the thoughts and mood that had led to the hangover. Until now, Harvey had classed himself as an occasional drinker. In fact, he totally enjoyed a glass of red, particularly a good pinot, and was fond of a smooth blended Scotch. He wasn't part of the new-age band of pompous Scotch drinkers who need to impress everyone with their knowledge of obscure single malts. He simply liked a large glass of Chivas with a pile of ice and a comfortable chair. And sometimes a glass became several when he needed to stop thinking quite so much.

Last night he'd come home by about 7.30pm, happy to have reached the end of a stressful week and aware that there were still things needing to be tidied. He had that unsatisfied incompleteness that invaded his brain when he hadn't resolved an issue to his satisfaction. He'd attacked the situation with a left-over half-bottle of rather good Burgundy – to no avail, and after a bachelor comfort meal of eggs and beans, he battled on with the whiskey and a bad movie that he turned off half way through.

His thinking flitted from case to case. Though he tried to placate himself by saying that healthcare wasn't always ideal. The system wasn't perfect. Yet he also knew that these days the system usually owned up to its issues and had ways to deal with problems openly and effectively. He couldn't fathom why these cases were different and why he was having difficulty progressing these conversations. He kept looking for connections between the cases, between the EMS and the hospital issues, between the intelligence from the health department about their focus on good news, and Fenland's blunt warnings. Harvey couldn't bring this all together in a way his brain could accept. Why did all of these issues all emerge in a cluster?

As is the way, though, a couple of drinks and more circular thoughts led to a vortex of negative contemplation that spiralled to a useless point close to the bottom of the bottle.

Harvey lay on his sofa and drifted back to sleep, awakening a couple of hours later with clarity of mind that he didn't deserve. There was something he could do and there was no doubt he needed to act. Harvey knew that if he ignored this situation or did nothing to get the ball rolling towards a resolution, it would continue to infect his brain.

Before he started the email, Harvey reminded himself that this was a draft and vowed to read it twice and wait half a day before sending it. Nothing angry, nothing impetuous, everything considered and balanced. This needed to be carefully stated. He'd been warned. It needed to come from the right place – his real concern for these patients and for the safety of the health system. It couldn't be allowed to be attacked as 'inflammatory' or 'reactionary' clinician ranting. It couldn't be allowed to be diminished by labelling it 'shroud-waving' – a term the insensitive and dismissive managers loved to use when scorning clinician concerns over possibly preventable patient deaths.

He showered then went to his desk and started the email to Fenland, copied to the CEO, Roger Hutten. He knew this was more than just sharing the joy. By doing this he was effectively sharing responsibility and accountability with the hospital executive, which couldn't be denied or ignored. If they needed a burning deck to inspire action then this could be it.

He started with a brief recap and outline of the three cases and the EMS Mastenyl issue and went on to advise that the State Forensic Institute and Coroner were in the process of reviewing these cases as part of standard reporting mechanisms. He also advised that he'd formally reported the asthma case and the Mastenyl tampering case to the EMS quality team for investigation. As a result, all the cases would soon come to open attention, with bodies required to start open and transparent investigations. Harvey went on to explain his concerns about the underlying systems problems ...

'It appears the underlying cause of the fatal outcomes in the first two inpatient cases is lack of resource, that is funding, to provide appropriately skilled staff, effective supervision of junior staff and efficient processes of care.

'Regarding the EMS issues presented, these go to the core cultural problems and lack of commitment of parts of that profession to effective, proper and timely patient care. They suggest a cultural misdirection, which has come to focus excessively on the development of interventional paramedicine, and advancement of that profession, rather than best patient outcomes.

The issue of abuse of narcotic agents in the EMS, which appears widespread, is a major concern; however, the ineffective organisational response to this unethical and criminal behaviour is reprehensible.

Of greatest concern is a palpable reduction in the transparency and openness with which our whole State health system is prepared to review and analyse incidents. Lack of compliance with State reporting legislation regarding sentinel critical events through Health Department reporting and Root Cause Analysis is extremely problematic.

Failure to report defined cases to the Coroner, together with provision of reports in which crucial information is withheld, may be open to criminal action.

It is my view that these issues, when seen as a whole, potentially describe a failure of governance standards of serious proportions and I advise that, in my opinion, these matters should be escalated to Board, Health Department, and Government levels'.

Ouch, Harvey knew this would stir the pot and was going to be recognised by management as directly critical of their roles and performance.

Was he concerned about the reaction to his email? Not really. He knew he'd tried all the standard escalation methods without response and that he was dropping the match that starts the fire.

Two hours later, he reread his email for the fourth time and then hit the send button. It left him with a feeling of completion and a touch of anxiety. What choice did he have – whistleblowing straight to the Health Department, leaking information to the press? Neither gave his hospital the chance it should have to address and repair these problems, but both would have been spectacularly effective. If he went public, Harvey figured he would have at least the short-term protection that comes with public visibility. Either way, he suspected any reaction he generated would not be good for his career.

He sat for a while, reflecting on the whole scenario. He could have focussed on himself and spent time lamenting the fact that he was in an unpleasant place and had found himself acting because the system or its governance was fragmented. He could have sat there asking himself, 'Why should I bother? Why not just walk away?' He could have said this situation was just down to the Huttens and Fenlands of the world and let them drown in the shit they had caused.

Much better to stay angry, he thought. Much better to stay alive and interested in fixing the damn mess. Harvey didn't see himself as a zealot or an evangelist – he just believed in right and wrong, with not much in between.

The downside to caring was the expenditure of his reserve of emotional energy, the anger and frustration that came with it and the sense of failure when he was unable to put things right. Harvey was a 'fixer'; he didn't like to see the job half done, or people being hurt just because the system was permitted to remain broken. But he also needed to stay on top of this type of stress so he could get on with the day-to-day, live his life happily. Survive.

A game of tennis and lunch with Rob and Jess would help all that.

Unfortunately, Harvey discovered that the excess energy from worry does not convert to physical energy, and Rob walked on him on the court. The hangover, residual sleep deficit, mild gastritis and dehydration didn't help. Despite the loss, Harvey felt more virtuous for the exercise and clearer in the head.

The three headed off to Noshry for lunch and sat on the decking in filtered autumn sunlight. Harvey felt the pure tastes of a calamari-Asian-fusion-salad-slaw-thing doing him good. The salty soy and cleansing power of wasabi obliterated the last of his hangover effectively. It was appropriate, therefore, that he and his comrades found themselves sitting after lunch with a 'cleansing', crisp Sauvignon Blanc from New Zealand, talking their way into a long afternoon.

Harvey shared little of his mood from earlier. With Jess and Rob he found it easier to be positive and more analytical than when he tried to wrestle alone with his thoughts. The bouncing of ideas and testing of conspiracy and other theories was way more effective with more than one brain involved.

Rob had met up with an old pal from his union days just the night before, and, although not close friends, they had always managed to catch up every six months or so to trade family and work stories over a beer or three. From this conversation, Rob believed that he understood a little more behind the current game, but as is the way with beer-fuelled sessions, hops and malt can dilute the reliability of information.

'Harvey, I'm not absolutely certain if I got this right, but Bill was basically saying that the whole political space is feral now, with positioning and posturing for the election in July. Bill now works in government, in industrial relations, and says that the corridors are heaving with gossip and theories – his self-confession was that probably half of what he'd heard was accurate. Having said that, if half of that half is true, then there is some serious badness going on, and we can stop believing we are just conspiracy theorists.'

Rob went on to paint a picture, which Harvey absorbed word by word.

'So, the talk is that the government is down by a couple of million in terms of funding for this election campaign. Step up

Health Minister Christine Henderson who is said to have some close and personal connections with the construction industry and an interest in moving out of the unpleasant and politically unwinnable bottomless pit of the health ministry. It's rumoured that her venture-capitalist husband, although a bit older, is a sucker for an extremely attractive power-woman and has been more than helpful with campaign funds and connections. The walls are whispering that by 'coincidence' not only will this ambitious Health Minister move post-election to the happier portfolio of business and planning, but that previously reluctant political donors in the construction business will be reaching deeply into their pockets, thereby solving a large and looming problem.

Now, as one minister moves on, another person would need to be promoted into the vacancy created. Enter Jane Chantier, our revered and ruthless current Secretary for health, and wife of your unpopular CEO.'

'So,' said Harvey, 'the government survives, and the Health Minister moves up on the crest of a wave of dirty money from someone whose favours she will be in a position to repay. The void she creates is filled by Hutten's psychopath wife. And the connection to our issue is what?'

Jess added quickly, 'Harvey, the connection is good news. Elections are won by good news and government spending, so there's a strong interest in not having scandals, criticism or failure of programs the government is behind. For instance the EMS practice developments. These are big winners for the public who only get to see the good news side of the story. No one wants to provide the opposition with fuel to fight the election – they need to silence any talk of health system failings, whether in pre-hospital, ED or the wards. There is a lot of motivation to showcase government investment in health systems – and the construction industry would be more than happy to hear about almost a half billion in building works. Hmmm, I wonder who will be picking up those contracts and which politicians may need to be influenced to make all the right pieces of the story align?'

Harvey continued the thread ... 'And which ambitious Government Departmental Secretary and CEO husband we all love and respect might work with relevant unions and organisational leaders to make sure that the health side of the good news story is not disturbed by tawdry issues like drug scandals and preventable deaths – all in the public interest of course.'

'The thing is,' Rob said, 'this is a whole lot bigger than a couple of hospital or EMS managers wanting to look good or to cover their arses. If Bill is even vaguely right, then I think this is unbeatably big and we need to think extremely carefully about getting any closer to it. If the construction industry is coughing up money, it's pretty unlikely to be coming from a collection of high integrity benevolent donors ... ' Rob shifted uncomfortably. 'What options do we have? We have a pile of rumour, no way to verify anything, really, and so no way to take any action other than the restating of what we know – that bits of our systems are stuffed, that patients are getting harmed and that some of our staff are both criminals and victims of this.'

You're right,' said Harvey. 'We don't have and won't be able to get anything solid to put on the table. All we have is routine channels to escalate through and we know they'll squash everything we raise. This is truly stuffed. We could go the official whistle-blower route, but we know the risks attached to that. We could go the press-leak route, which is guaranteed to back-fire in our faces.'

'We could go work in Hobart,' offered Jess.

They both turned to her with looks of amusement. Her suggestion that this may not be a fight worth having and that life might be much simpler and more pleasant if they withdrew from this space hadn't entered either of their heads.

Chapter 15

Cut the Crap - SUFFICIENCY

Harvey behaved himself that night and woke on Sunday in a more constructive frame of mind, which was fortunate because he needed to get to work on his next podcast. The day was conducive to creativity with the sky bright and his garden framed in the large window in front of his desk – a colourful melange of red and golden foliage. He watched two birds busily building a nest with impressive collaboration and efficiency. Turning to his computer, he imagined he was in a small auditorium with an attentive audience and started his next conversation ...

In my earlier podcasts, I explored the need for truth and constructive confrontation, and how we might approach these ideas. Today I will delve into the concept of sufficiency and how this has such a profound impact on our lives and our world. Perhaps this is a useful beginning step towards a different approach for the future.

SUFFICIENCY.
I asked a group of people in an efficiency workshop some time ago, 'How many lives do you have to live?' Apart from a lonely Buddhist, the answer from the group was a consistent 'one'. I asked the same group, 'How many inhabitable planets are you aware of?'

Now even the Buddhist agreed that there was only one. So, I asked them next, 'Given that you probably have only one experience of time on this single earth that needs to provide for your children and future generations, how much time and how much resource is it OK to waste?'

One can be tempted to fall into a logic trap and answer that it makes no sense to waste any time or resource at all – but that response fails to acknowledge the inherent imperfection of the human condition.

So, some waste may be all right? Let's say we minimise waste or tolerate unavoidable waste… But what is unavoidable? How much wasted time is too much? How much wasted matter or product is too much? Unfortunately, my workshop group were unable to help… there are no easy answers to these questions!

Japan's largest company, Toyota, has created a whole culture in its approach to production and quality, which we know as Lean Thinking. This method and philosophy revolve in large part around the elimination of waste. At a more spiritual level, both Shinto, through its respect of the spirit of all objects (kami), and Buddhism, through release from suffering and attachment to the excesses of the material world, have much to say about waste and valuing our resources.

So, we can look at sufficiency from the perspective of a philosophy, which respects that all of what we have is in a way precious and so should not be fritted away – neither time nor substance. There is a purity to this thought that is also simple and intuitive. We can also look at waste from the perspective of balance. How can it be right for us to be wasteful when much of the world suffers with insufficiency?

If we wish to be purely utilitarian, we can acknowledge that to be most efficient we must avoid waste.

The simple and logical conclusion that we should avoid waste wherever possible is attractive and I would suggest non-contentious. Then why do we have and allow so much waste? Do we not see the waste around us? Do we not appreciate our time is being wasted? Why do we not have a sensitivity to waste? I will come back to these questions.

There is no shortage of ways to think about waste. I would be happy to wager that anyone listening to me now could think of a handful of examples of waste in their lives within the next ten seconds! When I asked my workshop group to spend ten minutes talking among themselves to produce labels for classifying waste, they came back with only three groups. This is essentially the same result I have met in many groups and it seems to define the common way we think about waste.

Effort, Time and Things are the three types of waste I will focus on.

If I expend more energy than is necessary to accomplish something, I have wasted effort. If I am doing something valueless, this is also a waste of energy. The return on the expenditure of energy is disproportionately lower than the gain. The inefficiency of a process itself, or the value of the effort in comparison to the value of the outcome, defines the waste.

If I lose time by delay or waiting in a queue or by reworking or repeating something that was wrong or substandard or defective, I have wasted time.

If I have things, which I do not need or have a reasonable use for, then this is also a type of waste. Of course, this could occur through over-production as a manufacturer or through excessive acquisition as a consumer.

The most wasteful items comprise elements of all three types of waste. For example, the production of excessive quantities of something of little value, which is commonly defective.

It's not hard to work out that you are being wasteful (through excess) when you can't stuff any more clothes or shoes into your cupboards because they are already full. If you look at those items bulging out of your cupboards and think about the last time they were used, then even a microgram of insight will tell you that you're being wasteful. What stopped you from being content with sufficient, not excess?

Think about what goes out in your rubbish bin each week – how much food do you waste? Hopefully, these days, not so much. Think instead of the food that goes into the rubbish bin in the bowels of a large hotel or which expires on the shelves of the supermarket and ends up as refuse.

Think about things we consume that we don't need to, and which don't add value to our lives – much of the food we eat is like this, many of the cosmetics we use are like this, and nearly all of the homeopathic pills we pop can be thought of this way. We have become addicted to using the next cool thing, taking the next super remedy, consuming the next fad food … because of the way we are, and because of the way our society works.

These things are not new to our world, and, despite being shameful, we haven't changed our approach to them, perhaps because waste and excess are so ingrained in our culture. In our attempts to remedy this we have developed huge movements and social awareness actions to stem the tide – we look to gurus to tell us how to declutter and organize our houses, because we don't have whatever it takes to stop for two seconds and work that out for ourselves. I would have thought that the average human could look at their cupboard and see that it was heaving and make a decision to do something about it! However, if learning to roll items instead of folding and hanging, and having boxes in drawers, and believing in possessions sparking joy is what it takes, then the commitment to a methodology with mantras and rituals may be just what we need. The decluttering movement has much to offer. Ridding ourselves of the excess cluttering and complicating our lives may well help us transition to a simpler, quasi-minimalistic existence.

These examples are relatively banal and hardly earth shattering at the individual level; however, when multiplied by the population of the earth, particularly the affluent societies, this assumes phenomenal proportions. The fact is that when we look beyond these homegrown examples, we see exactly the same thing everywhere and, interestingly, in the workplace or commercial world, the way that waste or excess is viewed is even more casual. If it's not my money being spent, do I care how many widgets are used in a process, whether at the end of the day I discard a thousand unsold food items, whether electrical energy is consumed wastefully by leaving uncountable numbers of appliances in stand-by power mode or if I fill a stock room with enough supplies for a year? Probably not.

So, to move from the tangibly wasted things to wasted effort. This is really where we construct processes – or ways of doing things – that simply create churn. Churn is doing things that don't contribute efficiently to a useful output. A useful output is something we need to produce, something that is required, something that has or adds value to our world. Unfortunately, the ways we produce these items is often wasteful. Churn is doing things that do not contribute to a useful output.

This waste can sit in the structures around the process – for example the 'bureaucracy' can be intrinsic to the process. Bureaucracy is that joyful pile of crap we encounter when dealing with formal departments or large organizations; it is characterized by rules and regulations that define things that must be done despite them adding little or no value. Filling out forms, re-filling the same form, providing a useless report every month, which nobody looks at, complying with rules and process steps (because there is no other way allowed) until enough time passes that the original goal is lost, bypassed or forgotten. OMG, don't we all love that experience – doesn't it leave us feeling pleased that our taxes have been spent in this way?

NO!

Of course, there is always the option to revolt and refuse to play the game that the bureaucracy demands. But this strategy will take you in dichotomous directions – either the door will close and you will not progress one inch without compliance or no one will even notice what you're doing and you will do what you wanted to in blissful invisibility ... At the heart of it, the bureaucracy didn't really care about what you were aiming to do, just that you did it their way... and filled in all the forms, in triplicate!

Bureaucracy exists to create useless jobs for people who would otherwise fill a useful job. It is essentially a tax or fee-based employment strategy for a bunch of people who, in the end and through no fault of theirs directly, contribute nothing much to the world. At the centre of bureaucracy is a need for society to regulate. This is probably a reasonable need. However, rather than approaching this efficiently as perhaps a private sector organisation would do, similar tasks become complex reworked machinations of a system steeped over time in self-interest and nepotism. The truly weird aspect of this is that even the people working within a bureaucracy know it's stuffed, know how it could be improved, but are powerless to change it. The bureaucracy is just classic 'cut the crap'.

Duplication is a special process churn simply due to lack of process design. In other words, when processes are allowed to develop without mapping and design, duplication is risked. With correct process architecture, duplication should almost never exist.

The most common form of duplication is seen in process steps, which, when repeated, create not only certain waste, but the potential for error. In my world of medicine, the likelihood of a hospital patient escaping duplication is zero.

Error is a particular flavour of churn, which is slightly different. Yes, it does result in waste as we rework something that was erroneous, but if we assume that error is due to mistake not poor design of a process, then it is inevitable in human systems. We often focus on the apparent waste associated with error, but we all understand that error is inevitable. It is usually due to unintentional deviation from a correct method. The real opportunity with error is to learn by understanding why it occurred – to learn something that may reduce the risk of future human error. The bigger waste is to waste the opportunity to learn and improve from the error. Eliminating error is a prime way to ensure the resource we expend is sufficient to achieve our goal and is not wasted in fixing the problems we have created through mistakes.

So, let's look at a couple of areas where we aren't making errors, but create waste by being too productive. This is the concept of goal-overshoot and is a trap we can fall for because of our natural desire to 'get it right'. In my Brussels colloquium, I gave the example of marathon running ... Who needs to run a marathon? No one needs to be fit enough to run a marathon, and many people have been injured or died in training or during a marathon. Surely the healthy benefits of fitness would be obtained by people running five or ten kilometres at most. In the same way, pursuit of perfection in general is wasted effort and amounts to delusional aspiration. Is the pursuit of perfection noble or wasteful? Is it excessive to set an unattainable goal thus wasting resource?' Instead, I'm proposing a goal of sufficiency or excellence, which is somewhere short of perfection, is rational and satisfactory, and not associated with a waste of additional unrewarded effort and resource. The difference and benefit between sufficiency and perfection are often marginal, often imperceptible and often irrelevant.

It is curious that much of the waste in our lives goes unnoticed. The great exception is the waste of time. Perhaps because it is so precious to all of us, we seem to notice when time fritted away.

Time wasting is tricky. Like error, it is inevitable, but time is a single-use product – we never get it again. We need to get the perspective right when it comes to using time. We need to invest our time wisely only in valuable pursuits.

Some espouse the thinking that 'the past is gone, and the future has not yet arrived, therefore live for now'. Sounds profound, but sells short the value of time as an investment. It makes sense to invest time in the past so as not to waste the learning. Investing in thinking about the future also makes sense if it leads to a better future. Wasting time in rumination on the past and re-thinking things that are unchangeable makes no sense. In the same way spending time on unrealistic future plans (AKA fantasy) is wasteful.

What doesn't make sense is overt time-wasting inflicted on us. No system ever worked better because someone designed unnecessary delays, queues or waiting. When these are present efficiency has been compromised or in other words a system or process is simply not right. As a result, time will be wasted, secondary delays will occur in processes dependent on the output of the first step, and production cost will increase. If it happens that you are the widget moving through this process, then it is also your time wasted by the delay or queue, and don't we always have something better to do than sit in a queue? If you are unlucky and the delay is in your access to health care, then you may lose more than your time or your money. All around the world, emergency department patients are spending too long queued on trolleys waiting for access to care. In the same way, every public health system has unacceptable waiting lists for patients in need of important surgical interventions. A significant proportion of these people will have worse outcomes or die because of unnecessary delays in their care.

But it's not all about being the victim of time wasters – it is likely that we waste more of our own time than anyone else does. We commonly do this by displacement of tasks through procrastination. Oh, that uncontrollable (or maybe sometimes controllable) need to not start or not finish something. And aren't we fortunate to exist in this millennium, when the selection of electronic ways to procrastinate or waste our own time is just so voluminous.

If we were to believe that nobody deliberately aims to be wasteful or to use more than is sufficient, then we must accept that we have an inner drive that pushes us towards excess.

Perhaps the potential to waste is just part of our makeup, but that doesn't make it OK for us to simply ignore it. In some countries thirty per cent of food production is wasted. In some countries people starve to death regularly.

The solution is to look for and find balance in all things. We need to shift that culture of greed – 'more is better' – and the belief that more is safer or will provide security. We need to replace it with awareness that 'my waste is someone else's insufficiency' or is a lost resource or foregone time that the world will never have again. The fundamental change required is the acceptance of and commitment to the ideas of limitation and moderation, of sufficiency.

Attachment to the concept of 'more' is a huge threat to our world. If we replaced our current excesses and waste with responsible, considered consumption then we would be mindful and vocal about this on a daily basis. The way this will happen will echo many of the changes that humankind has seen in entrenched wrongs of the past. People will think, discuss, share ideas and they will speak out. Then change will happen. This type of populist movement has worked for all of the major social corrections that the human race has achieved – why not something as obviously destructive as waste!

Waste is just another form of crap that we have allowed to invade and threaten our lives, so we need to find a way to remove it and accept sufficiency. We can help each other do that if we are prepared to speak up and 'cut the crap'.

It was late afternoon by the time Harvey had checked and edited his script, emailed it to Elli and made himself another Earl Grey. The weather was fine, the days had started to shrink, a task had been ticked, and he was happy with the way his thoughts had come together. He settled on his terrace with his Sunday newspaper, sinking into his Adirondack and vowing not to nod off for at least 15 minutes.

The paper led with stories about reductions in unemployment in the construction sector on the back of booming public sector building contracts. Try as he might to escape yesterday's hypothesising, he couldn't – so the prospect of a late afternoon snooze in the sun was replaced by wondering about who was up to what, and how much damage to the health system would be tolerated in the name of electioneering, political ladder climbing, and sweetening the profit lines of a well-connected and unpleasant group of construction heavies.

Harvey knew many people who had spent a lifetime career in public sector health, pushing, dragging, carrying it forward. This sort of behaviour would hurt them.

Chapter 16

Monday 15 April 2019

'Good morning Elli – or good evening for you in Europe somewhere, answered Harvey.

'Hello Harvey, I'm in Barcelona at the European Resuscitation Council conference – good weather, good tapas, a little sangria… life's tough! Thanks for sending through your script, I love it, and we need to record it for next weekend. We need to keep feeding your fans.'

'Ha-ha! 'I don't think I have a lot of fans around Sydney right now.'

'I'm not sure what you're on about, Harvey, but I can give you some news on the podcasts. We had the first lot of useful analytics come through today and the news is incredibly good. I think Brussels with its big professional audience and the initial real-time webcast has triggered interest and press. It seems to have primed the social media space, and the release of the first three podcasts was anticipated by a lot of interested people.' Elli sounded excited. 'Bottom line is that we have just over 42,000 subscribers in the first three weeks. Harvey, your talk from Brussels seems to be pushing buttons. The other thing we are seeing is good growth in download numbers, which is fantastic.'

'Thanks Elli, I can't pretend to know what that mean, but I'll take the lead from your tone. It all sounds positive.'

'Harvey, it's not positive; it's spectacular. There's something in your message which people are connecting with and I think it's the quite simple and slightly rude mantra you are tagging this all with.

Harvey, I've had a request from our PR people to get you in front of some press. An interview or two and some morning TV chat appearances would be helpful. I think Jill from our Melbourne office will be in touch about a press release and interview for tomorrow or Wednesday – I hope that's all OK?'

Harvey didn't quite know how to respond. This wasn't what he'd expected and international notoriety wasn't going to make life any simpler in Sydney.

'Wow,' he replied, 'I guess that all sounds good, and, yes, I'll wait for the call. I should be able to work something out, but I'm on ED shifts this week also.'

Elli let a chuckle trickle down the line. 'Harvey, I don't think you get it – if this keeps going, you're going to have a potential audience of hundreds of thousands, and it's likely you'll become public property. Look, I must get back to the function I'm at, but I'll see if I can swing a trip out to Sydney next week. I think we need to have a chat about your trajectory.'

'OK,' Harvey said. 'That sounds like a plan. Talk later'

Trajectory. Hmm that sounded painful and difficult to control. Harvey collected his thoughts for a few minutes, digesting the news and wondering whether the idea of his personal view of the world going viral was a good thing or not. Things he'd published in the past had received a standard constrained academic enthusiasm at best, a few conference presentations, radio interviews from time to time. This was a different ball game. A research paper was one thing – a hypothesis, a method, some measurement, some conclusions. All precise, controlled, factual. Cut the crap was none of those things. It was his thinking, his way of living, surviving, reacting, and now it was out there, completely public.

What Harvey hadn't realised was that the train had already left the station and he was on it. By the end of the day he would hear from Loquitur's west coast office, and by lunchtime tomorrow he would have completed interviews with local press and radio and have a current affairs TV interview scheduled for Tuesday evening. This seemed to be a bullet train.

Leaving his office, he headed down to the ED to start his shift, consciously resetting his brain to the clinical world and the challenges he would face over the next hours. It was a useful strategy. This figurative switch-throw allowed him to move from one intellectual world to another. Employed by clinicians everywhere, it provided a way to concentrate on critical issues without allowing distraction and then, at the end, to turn off the harshness of that space and allow a real life. That was the theory anyway. For Harvey, the former mechanism worked much better than the latter, and his work invaded his private space, as is the way of things.

His thought compartmentalisation worked well for a couple of hours until Alex called him just before lunchtime.

'It seems you have caused some consternation with your email last week,' said Alex 'and we have been 'invited' to a meeting with Hutten and Fenland on the tenth floor this afternoon. Should be interesting.'

'I can't say I'm totally surprised,' replied Harvey. 'I didn't intend them to ignore it. The issues are real and dangerous. Given some of the bigger picture stuff going on, it's going to be interesting to see what angle they take.'

'I'm not quite sure what you mean Harvey – what bigger picture stuff are you on about?'

'Let's just say the 'political environment',' Harvey said. 'Just some things I've been hearing that suggest this may all be part of a bigger game.'

'Be careful,' advised Alex, 'we need to be up there by four, so call round to my office before that.'

'OK.' Harvey headed back to the ED, working through his shift, trying to keep his mind on the job.

As he walked to Alex's office later that afternoon, he received an SMS from Phil Vancleef at the Coroner's office:

<Re Cardiac Case – Coroner has listed for investigation and Hosp has been asked for revised statement. Re EMS, etc., Coroner's officer is investigating with view to refer for judicial review... FYI & Confidential Best, Phil>.

Interesting. No doubt this would cause some jitters on the upper floors. Harvey amused himself by picturing a herd of cats getting among the pigeons.

―√╱╲―√╲―

Just as Harvey and Alex were taking a seat in the tenth-floor meeting room with its stunning harbour views, Roger Hutten and Todd Fenland entered the room. It seemed the mood would be direct, with no hand shaking or preliminary small talk today.

Fenland started with what felt like a scripted and rehearsed introduction.

'Harvey, thank you for making time this afternoon to meet with us. I understand from your email on Friday that you have some concerns that we would like to address with some urgency. Perhaps before we do that, however, I'd like to reiterate that we do have standard mechanisms for investigating clinical outcome concerns and it is important that all our staff, no matter how serious their concerns and no matter how senior they are, work through those mechanisms. It is unhelpful to receive inflammatory and hyperbolic emails directed to senior executives when the in-house mechanisms for review and intervention are adequate.'

'I think part of the point was that those mechanisms were not –' Harvey said. Fenland kept talking over him.

'If you would let me finish, Professor Pearce, and we can come back to discussion later. The fact is that the email you directed to me and the CEO last week was purely your opinion, drew extensive conclusions, and recommended escalation of the matters you raised – independent of any other internal process and without consideration of any internal investigations that may be going on. I want to make it quite clear that this is not the way we expect to receive information and that there are appropriate channels of communication and escalation.'

'I'm sorry, but I do need to interrupt you here, Todd,' began Harvey. 'I did raise these matters through usual channels, and I did escalate my concerns both through the relevant committees prior to writing to you. There is no certain mechanism for raising my concern about the system level issues where I said …' Harvey opened the email on his phone to read ' … there is a palpable reduction in the transparency and openness with which we are prepared to review and analyse incidents. Lack of compliance with State reporting legislation regarding sentinel critical events through Health Department reporting and RCA is extremely problematic.' Harvey put down the phone.

'This and the issue I raised about the EMS are not issues that lend themselves to standard, local, internal review. Furthermore, I believe they are a hospital – and system-level of risk, which I assumed should be escalated to the highest levels. This is why I have escalated them to yourselves.'

Alex weighed in to the discussion. 'Roger, I'm with Harvey on this. There is a strong feeling among clinical staff here at Queens that we have been raising concerns about resourcing and safety processes for months with little engagement from executive.'

Hutten moved in his seat, effectively signalling that it was his turn to speak, and provided his best attempt at a face of concern and solidarity. His words would be correct and yet unbelievable.

'We appreciate your concerns… We understand your motivation… We know you have the best interests of … We value your view of the big picture …' He continued droning on … 'Sensitivity of the government and health department … Potential of the press to exaggerate … Damage to reputations and prospects … Need for certainty, not simply clinician's conclusions … '

'Professor Pearce, I do share your concerns, and I also share the view that Mr Fenland has expressed reasonably bluntly. We don't need nor do we benefit from inflammatory email, and the best way to avoid these is for us to be more active and effective in our communication with clinical staff like yourself. Your frustration is no doubt a reflection on our lack of effective provision of information and in failing to involve you in the improvement strategy we have in the pipeline.'

Really? thought Harvey. Does he actually expect me to believe this?' He tried to keep a straight face but felt his eyebrows migrating north.

'I am absolutely committed to resolve these issues,' said Hutten. 'And I cannot think of anyone more motivated or capable to help in that work than you, Harvey.'

'Well, of course I am happy to do my part and I'm more than happy to continue my input into the hospital and health department committees, but to be honest, I've been frustrated by the inability of these mechanisms to get traction.'

'I know,' continued Hutten. 'I sensed this earlier, and I want you to consider approaching this from a different angle. I would like you to set up and run a small taskforce for our health service to formally review our clinical governance systems and to look collaboratively at any relevant components of partner organisations such as the EMS.

We need something at a whole organisation level, which has full executive support to work through a structured process and deliver us a set of recommendations and interventions we can take to the government with the support of our board. I think we are talking an eight-to-ten-week consultation and review process, and a month for board review before we take a paper to the health department.

'Of course, we'll provide you with a team, some project staff, resources and funds, and access to any committees and records you need. Harvey, we appreciate your skills and we also appreciate your ability as a leader among our clinical staff. People listen to you and respect you, and it seems this is now starting to be the case in the big world – your podcasting appears to be remarkably successful. If Alex can work it in the ED, with a replacement consultant, I'd like you to come on to the exec team for the next three to four months to work this through. We'll see where things go from there. What do you say?'

Well fuck me sideways, was what he thought. He managed to get his brain to filter that to, 'Let me have a think on this one if that's OK? Alex and I will need to talk it through, and I'd better have a look at the terms of reference for the taskforce. Can I get back to you in the next day or so?'

'Of course, of course.' Hutten smiled and sat back in his seat. 'You know, we're all on the same side here, and we'd be most enthusiastic for you to be fully on board. Here's my mobile number – give me a call anytime.'

Chapter 17

Persuasion

Harvey rode the elevator down with Alex, thinking over his pressured exasperation from last Friday and wondering just where it connected with this conversation with Hutten and Fenland. They retreated to Alex's office and sat facing each other across the desk.

'Well do me sideways and call me Sally,' said Alex in a rare moment of profanity that made Harvey smile and wonder if Alex had read his mind. It wouldn't be the strangest thing that had happened today …

'What do you make of it?'

Harvey couldn't decide whether he'd just been thanked and temporarily promoted or whether he'd been handed a poisoned chalice. 'I don't know for sure,' Harvey replied, 'but a big part of me is concerned. What about you?'

Alex also thought for a moment before he answered. 'Harvey, I've worked as a departmental manager in this and other organisations for the best part of twenty-five years now. I think I've had seven or eight CEOs and twice that many managers and divisional heads. Out of all those I could name less than half a handful would I trust to do the right thing ahead of looking after their own prospects.

People in these jobs are transient parasites; they are promotion-seeking toadies, by and large, and are always on the upward move, leaving a trail of careless wreckage behind them. They live in a world decorated by perverse incentives, which are irresistible. I have never known how to work with them to achieve what we need to for the patient and our health system.' Alex was on a roll.

'So, are they being genuine? I don't know, but probably not. Is this an opportunity to achieve something? I'd say yes. Will it end up with a result that you will be happy with? Maybe.'

Harvey held Alex in high esteem and had always valued his ideas and insights, and this situation was no different. He hadn't shared any of the detail of Rob's intelligence with Alex, so from the point of view of politics and murky motivations he assumed that Alex was in the dark. His assessment was generous, thought Harvey.

'Alex, I agree. Every part of that discussion made my skin crawl. There are a dozen different ways they could deal with what I raised without involving me at all, and as for running the Spanish Inquisition over three months – you know I doubt whether we'd even scratch the surface with the EMS stuff from here at Queens. The paramedics won't let us near the real issues, and I suspect we'll be left holding a handful of unanswerable questions. As for the issues here – I'm sure Fenland would be fully across them already. The real question is whether, by working from within their camp, I can get enough light on the issues to move the agenda along? And why do they want to risk me shedding light on their governance and systems issues – perhaps they think they will appear selfless, soul-baring, problem-facing new-age executives if they drive improvement no matter what the risk to their personal reputations… unless, of course, it doesn't matter to them?'

'What do you mean?' said Alex.

'I'm not certain,' replied Harvey, 'but given the timeline they're proposing of three to four months – perhaps their worlds will be quite different by then?'

Alex looked at him, puzzled and slightly peeved, but Harvey wasn't ready to elaborate.

With a resolve to think on the offer overnight, Harvey left Alex and went back to his own office to tidy up the day. He picked up his email, which included a message from Elli about a press conference and radio interview for tomorrow. There was one from Hutten's assistant with the terms of reference of the taskforce review attached – that could wait till he got home and found a bottle of something to dilute it with.

There was another from the EMS professional standards unit telling him they'd received his reports and 'matters would receive due attention' and 'thankyou'. He felt certain that such a calm-water response was simply a template completed by a functionary – the organisational anxiety behind what he had raised would be animated, and he had no doubt that high-level conversations would have occurred already and would not have been calm or quiet. The next meeting of the EMS-ED Case Review Committee was only a fortnight away. They would table his report and the cases in an open forum, which included all of the city EDs and the health department. He knew it needed to happen, and drafted a quick email thanking the sender for the response and saying that the issue would also be listed on the agenda for the EMS-ED CRC at the end of the month. Then he added, 'Could you please ensure that detail and outcomes of any early investigation, and confirmation of police reporting, be provided to the committee?' Same cat, different flock of pigeons, he thought. Harvey went home.

He thought that the prospect of skipping a grade to the hospital executive club and getting an opportunity to play at the level where influence and change could happen would generate more internal energy and some level of intellectual buzz.

Instead, Harvey found the quietness of his house, the whirr of his thoughts and the potential mountain of work ahead to be sapping. Sometimes the prospect of the next big task seemed to hit him in the face like this and it would take a good sleep, a weekend off, a diversion, to allow him to shift the shadow away and get on with it. He knew this task was big and ugly – full of stories of misery, error, harm, death. Good people would be caught up in it, tangled in among the wreckage of politics and professional posturing, squashed by bureaucratic convolution and funding deficiency.

But the opportunity was there and if he didn't take it, he knew he would not feel right, not because he thought he was the only one capable of doing what needed to be done, but because he knew what was required, knew he had the skills and believed it was what he should do. What made this and all the other 'extra' jobs something that he 'must' do? Why the need to find a next cause, a new crusade all the time?

He knew there wasn't an answer because he had been in this place before. He knew this wave of thoughts would paralyse him for the evening, so better to do nothing and allow a dusk of empty disquiet to come and go. He sat waiting for sleep to come …

He must have drifted off just before dawn, waking at almost 8am feeling sharp and ready to go. Bizarre, he thought, what two or three hours' sleep can do. The alarm on his phone reminded him that he needed to get moving – Tuesday 16 April 2019, 09.30, Press Conf & Interview, Centennial Offices, Market St.

By 9.15am he was sitting in the lobby of the newspaper house sipping his second long macchiato and running through sound-bite prompts with Jill Spencer who had flown up from the Loquitur Melbourne office overnight.

Like most people, Harvey felt exposed in a press conference. The vulnerability of sitting in front of a group of professional question-askers who have no inhibitions about entering and rummaging about inside your head was plainly uncomfortable. All the same Harvey had been there before and, after listening through Jill's prepared introduction, which she handed out to the group, he was ready to engage. The idea of a clinician recommending the world Cut the Crap and take a new and simple approach to life's challenges seemed to resonate, so Harvey opened the door to his thoughts and theories, sharing his brand of non-preachy pragmatism ...

Why?

'Well I guess that's a good first question. I think this approach is just a pile of common wisdom that's come my way over a career of working and living in an interesting space. I think I paid attention to that space, and the ideas and constructs developed. Sharing thought has always been part of my life, so here we are.'

The basis?

'Hmm, do we need a basis to have a hypothesis to connect a series of strategies and ways of thinking? Do we have a basis for the alternative, which is to be as we were, a combination of thoughts and ideas and philosophies that came from where?'

Self-help?

'No this isn't self-help; it isn't something that belongs on an airport bookshelf. Cut the Crap asks us merely to listen to ourselves. To listen for that inkling that something is a fabrication, hollow, wasteful, without value, then to ask ourselves about the place that thing occupies in our life.'

The biggest messages?

'Wow that is a bit difficult, but again I think that listening to our own thoughts and assessments of our world and consciously asking ourselves about the value of our actions. Awareness of and engagement with the bigger picture; being happy to confront what needs to be improved. These are all important.'

Future Podcasts?

'Yes, as Jill said, there are two more for release. Simplicity and Integrity, and then I think that's it. I suspect by then I will have said all I have to say and I can crawl back into my hole!'

Chilled?

'I don't think of myself as chilled. I would say I am barely emotionally average and have my own demons – Cut the Crap is a way to deal with what I can.'

Messages about our Sydney health systems?

'Look, I think it's important to separate this work and the thinking behind it from my day-to-day work as an ED physician here in Sydney. The ideas behind these presentations are intended for bigger life issues – they aren't intended as disguised rockets to aim at the local health system. I would hope they are relevant in some way to most people.'

Crisis in our health services?

'I'm quite sure that subject is not on the running list for today and this might be a better question for the health department … '

The reporter from The Australian then stole the show with her final question. 'Professor Pearce: Perhaps you need to Cut the Crap yourself and tell us what you know about avoidable deaths, cover ups and broken investigation systems in our hospitals and ambulance service, which are problematic right here and now in Sydney?'

'Look, as is the case with any health system, there are imperfections and opportunities in ours, but there are systems in place that exist to detect and resolve problems and performance issues. To be honest, I'm aware of some current issues, but it is not my position or role to comment further on these.'

By the next day, when translated to news font and published, somehow this became:

HEALTH SYSTEM STANDARDS UNDER QUESTION

Internationally acclaimed academic, ED physician and well-known lifestyle podcaster, Professor Harvey Pearce, interviewed on the crest of a record-breaking podcast series release.

Professor Pearce confirmed he was aware of 'issues' related to the effectiveness of systems to detect and resolve problems of patient safety in our health system.

Professor Pearce declined to comment on widespread speculation that Sydney health systems are at risk following reports of a series of deaths, cover-ups, and system failures.

'Seriously Harvey, I'm a bit more than a little disappointed. I thought we were on the same page.' Fenland had wasted no time in calling Harvey the next morning. No doubt the health department had been on his case as soon as they noticed the page two article.

'I'm sorry Todd, but this is all out of context. My podcast producer called the press conference. It had nothing to do with local issues. The questions about Sydney were thrown in at the end without notice and my responses have been 're-fashioned', let's say, to support a line they were running.' Fuck the press, thought Harvey.

'Sounds like you've been used then, Harvey. Maybe we need to organise you a little media coaching.' And an egg sucking exercise for my grandma, thought Harvey.

'Sure,' he replied, 'sounds like fun. Listen, Todd, on a different topic, I've given Roger's offer from Monday afternoon some thought, and Alex and I have discussed it – I'm happy to come on board and see what I can do to help.'

'Good, good,' replied Fenland, 'I wasn't sure if you would take up the offer, but I'd like you to start next Monday. We can get the team together by then. Just lie low and avoid the press and, in future, I want you to check with our media team before you front the press at all. Why don't you take the rest of the week off and come in fresh next week? I'll see you then and we'll brief your team.'

Harvey knew he was being controlled. What did the hospital's PR guys have to do with his podcasting?

'OK,' he said, wondering what he'd got himself into. Though the idea of a couple of days off was attractive. It would give him a chance to work through his last two podcasts in peace and quiet, and he needed to catch up with a few people.

Chapter 18

Yes Minister

Todd Fenland wasted no time heading to Hutten's office at the end of the corridor, his eagerness to please his demanding boss reflected in an exaggerated and servile haste. More like a suite than an office, Hutten occupied the corner rooms capturing city and harbour views through over-sized windows – all impressively accessible from his oversized desk and the oversized couch – but then all this was necessary to house his oversized ego and oversized arse.

Fenland didn't particularly like Hutten, but knew he was a ticket to his next job. The connections he had through his wife and the networks he cultivated with the health minister would look after that aspect of the future.

The door was open. Fenland knocked and entered, Hutten looking up from the papers on his desk.

'Good morning, Roger – have you got five minutes?'

'Sure, Todd, come in. Give me two seconds to finish this report.' He scanned the rest of the document, signed and dated it and then laid it aside. 'Coffee?'

'No thanks, Roger. I just called by to let you know I've spoken with Pearce already. That stuff in the paper this morning was not good, but I think it was more about some savvy reporters fishing than him leaking.'

'You may be right. What did you do about it?' Hutten filled an espresso cup from the ridiculously red La Scala machine on his sideboard. 'Either way, I need to let Jane know. She lost her shit over breakfast when she read the report in The Australian.'

'I've given him the message,' Fenland said, 'and the usual rules about press engagement and clearing stuff with PR first. He's a feisty bastard, though, and I'm not sure how much sinks in. By the way, he's agreed to come on board.'

Hutten moved back to his desk and reached for the phone, dialling on speaker. 'Shut the door will you, Todd?'

Fenland obeyed.

Two rings and she answered. It was always two rings. 'DHS, Secretary Chantier's Office,' answered her assistant.

'Good morning, Clare. This is Roger. Is Mrs Hutten available?' The same droll line he always used.

'Yes, Mr Hutten, Ms Chantier is available, I'll connect you now.'

'Hi Rog.'

'Hi Jane, I've got you on speaker with Todd Fenland here, OK?' Hutten waited.

'Sure, so what's up with Pearce, have you guys sorted it?'

'Good morning, Ms Chantier.' Fenland was always deferential with the boss's wife. 'I'm sure Pearce understood the message, whether he follows our advice will become evident, I guess. All the same, he's agreed to come on board for the governance review, which will keep him occupied and inside the tent. How he will respond to a short leash is a bit difficult to predict.'

'OK, but I had one of the creepy strategic advisors that Henderson and the Premier listen to come in here this morning and suggest some more colourful solutions if this doesn't all settle down. I would really like another level of confidence – I don't want any more leaks, rumours, lies, truths or anything coming out of your clinicians, except the silent breath they exhale.'

'I understand, consider it done.' Fenland wasn't sure he could promise.

'See you tonight, Roger.' She hung up.

'So, what do you think?' asked Hutten.

Fenland wasn't sure what he meant. There didn't seem to be anything to think about. The department and the political string-pullers seemed to be clear on the message. But Hutten was waiting for a reply. 'I think we need to keep a lid on things for a while, if not forever. Presumably this is all pre-election stuff, but they're taking it very seriously.'

'There's more to it than that,' replied Hutten, 'and we need to be certain that lid is on tight. If we need to lose some people over this, it won't be the end of the world.' He looked at Fenland.

Fenland understood, and wasn't at all sad.

'Now,' continued Hutten, 'I need to make a move. The Minister needs a heads up on all this and a couple of other matters, so I need to get going. I'll call you later, thanks Todd.'

He was moving towards the door already, having picked up his jacket and keys with the rather pretentious gilt BMW fob. He paused for Fenland to catch up then ushered him out. He half turned to his assistant as he left and said to no one in particular that he'd be back in by 3pm. Clearly, his mind was elsewhere and anyone in his space may as well have been a fly on the wall.

He pushed through traffic on the drive over to the Minister's office, which took him through a leafy corner of the CBD and past the familiar historic sandstone buildings that made up much of the centre of this city. His pass got him preferential access to the underground car park where he pulled into the usual visitor's park. Taking the lift to the top floor he noticed his heart rate rise just a little and the tiniest bead of sweat appear on his lip. He was looking forward to this meeting.

Minister Christine Henderson's executive assistant acknowledged Hutten as he arrived, indicating with a slightly excessive flourish of his clearly metrosexual hand that he could go straight in. Jimmy had been with the minister for three years, was paid well above the award rate and was the epitome of discretion and confidence. Just the door-bitch she needed.

Henderson was leaning her firm but nicely curved arse on the desk as Hutten entered. He noticed the pose, as well as the profile of her more-than-attractive face, and the outline of her perfect breasts. He knew the pose was for him, not Jimmy, and closed the door behind him.

He took his time walking across the room. She didn't acknowledge him at first then turned around as he approached. His next step placed his right foot between hers. 'I'm here to give you a heads-up, Minister.'

She lifted her right hand to cup him, saying, 'I see that.' Her hand gripped him. He looked down as her breasts rose, then watched as her left hand lifted her skirt, following curves, crevices and some artistic trimming then beyond. She rubbed him in time with herself for just as long as was necessary for them both.

This was one version of her Ministerial protocol that both Hutten and Henderson enjoyed. The encounter finished as romantically as it had started. After all, there was business to be done.

After a glass of reasonable French fizz and ten minutes chilling on her couch, Hutten explained the morning's conversations with Fenland and his wife. Henderson shared his incomplete confidence that Harvey was going to behave or that Todd Fenland would manage to contain him.

'The thing is,' she said 'there are a couple of health services where people are starting to grumble and it's a worry that the press have latched on. Clinicians feed on each other's whinging. Whether it's Pearce or someone else, it's probably just a matter of time before the probing and talking gets more serious.'

'So, what's the answer?' asked Hutten

'I'm not sure yet,' replied Henderson, 'but I'm meeting up with the Premier and some connections later this evening and I suspect we'll thrash it out. It's not the first time a politician has had to come up with a pre-election diversion.'

'Maybe you could take out an Iranian terrorist leader or perhaps start a war,' quipped Hutten.

'Gosh, that sounds like federal politics. I didn't know you were so ambitious Roger ... no, I was thinking something smaller scale and quite local.'

Chapter 19

Cut the Crap - SIMPLICITY

Again, for Harvey, sleep did not come easily that night. Had he known the directions the city's political wheels were turning that night, his anxiety would have been worse.

He went out to his terrace, armed with a glass of red and a packet of cigarettes he kept for times like this. Once a smoker, always a smoker. Though he had 'given up' many years before, at times of greatest stress or internal mayhem he'd still retreat to the cloud of poisonous smoke to hide from the world. In between times Harvey would not touch them.

When he'd placated his compulsion and achieved nothing real by way of emotional benefit, he retreated to his study, determined to tackle 'Simplicity' tonight rather than lie in bed wondering about sleeping. He dragged himself to bed at about 2am feeling pleased at having completed a full draft of the next talk.

> Sadly, there are many examples where we as individuals increase the complexity of our lives. In some respects, this is a modern plague of compulsion that we find it hard to avoid. We overfill our time and overcommit our emotional energy and suddenly find ourselves over-thinking and over-analysing the predicament we find ourselves in. To escape this, we need to accept a simpler view

of our lives which frees us from the tangle of complexity – we make a sea change, a tree change or down size or de-clutter – to reduce the complexity in our world and to enjoy the pleasure of simplicity.

And before you scratch your head and say, 'But it's a complex world – computers, technology, science, biology' – I ask you: isn't there complexity inherent in all these things? Let me clarify. There are many aspects of our existence, which are necessarily complex, often in the scientific and technical sphere. There is no way to find cures for many diseases unless we work with the complexities of cellular biochemistry, genomics, biological transmitters and receptors. There is no way to manufacture and distribute the food we need as a society without complex farming production, distribution systems and retailing processes. At a 'big world' level, complex structures and processes are necessary, but complexity in our individual lives ('little world') is often damaging.

So, if 'big world' complexity is usually necessary and 'little world' complexity is better avoided, what about the 'middle world'? Perhaps this is where the biggest complexity problem lies – that space between the self-definable and the unalterable.

It would be ironic to turn a discussion of the value of simplicity into something complicated and convoluted, so let me untangle this topic. In my view complexity that doesn't add value to an experience or outcome is simply crap. An understanding of complexity helps us move toward simplicity.

Complexity describes the inter-relationship between large numbers of components, structures or processes. It is the opposite of simplicity. The inter-relationships may come in many forms, such as dependency, influence, direction, acceleration, slowing, improving quality, causing error or defects. Complexity isn't good or bad, it simply describes. Many complex systems are exceptionally reliable and effective and have positive outputs.

The design of many complex systems is deliberately and necessarily intricate. In these situations, the design complexity is required to achieve the desired endpoint. For example, a mission to the moon is complex at every level for particularly good reasons and is designed with knowledge and appreciation of its complexity.

Simple systems are inherently less risky and therefore are less error prone and more predictable. A complex system that is poorly or not-at-all designed and which has evolved organically or incrementally, fundamentally amplifies risk. Where excellent complex systems stand out is in the monitoring for and detection of deviation or small errors before they affect the desired outcome.

Just imagine: you have a newly diagnosed cancer and you need a life-saving procedure within two weeks.

Option a): you are assigned a case manager who has standard, scrutinised ways to interact with admissions, pharmacy, medical staff and labs to get you into hospital and operated on within a week. Simple!

Option b): The surgeon gives you a list of five departments and five phone numbers to navigate. Department A is over-run and cannot see you till next week. Department B does your tests for admission at once, but by the time you are admitted they are out-dated and need to be repeated. The clerk in pharmacy is having a dreadful day and your chemo will not be ready till three weeks, and someone forgot to tell the medical staff you were coming in next Friday and they scheduled someone else for the OR. Complex!

Where a complex system has many steps and relationships, it is intuitive that at each of these points of inter-relationship, there is the potential for error and for tension. So: more complex, more steps, more relationships, more risk, and inevitably more error. Unnecessary or poorly-managed complexity increases the likelihood of variable outcomes and unintended consequences because all the inter-relationships and inter-dependencies cannot possibly be monitored and controlled. The tensions between them consume resource rather than applying resource efficiently. Complexity is often one step or one error away from chaos.

On the other hand, simplicity, removes extraneous components of process or structure, reduces options, reduces variability, reduces the number of places where something can go wrong, and so trends towards reliability. Through reduction in steps and interplays, simplicity assists in uncovering the nature of a risk and resolving it.

The simpler system trends towards dichotomy and clarity in the ways we can describe it or think about it. The system is more likely to be: right or wrong, good or bad, effective or wasteful, profitable or not profitable, safe or dangerous, moral or immoral. Our knowledge of the system will be more reliable, as will the system itself. Complexity can disguise, through confusion and obscurity, the parts of a system that we need to see clearly if we are going to improve it.

With this knowledge we can also start to see why some complexity is driven by players with something to gain from it. Those who live to play power games, usually at middle-manager level, positively love complex systems in which small Machiavellian moves can easily and profoundly disrupt the systems and processes for honest players.

Complexity in relationships between structures, people, departments or processes drives a level of tension, which exists to be manipulated by power-players – to weaken or strengthen as they wish. Those who have bubbled to a position of seniority despite lack of capability or talent and find themselves in a role beyond their skillset also love complexity, because there's always a process or someone else to hide behind to mask shortcomings. One can always delegate, devolve responsibility, perform a review, call in a consultant... These lovers of complexity are often seen in hierarchical professions or industries, where they are promoted based on longevity and loyalty, and survive in shrouded spaces, protecting their self-interested world until pension time... Or until someone shines a light on them.

By increasing clarity and visibility, simplicity tends to expose perverse and non-aligned behaviour, 'games', inefficiency, incompetence and subversion.

The middle world is where most of us find ourselves butting heads with complexity. So how do we deal with this? What do we do to supply the clarity and visibility, the simplicity? The reality is that most of us have little direct influence. We go to work each day and are small cogs in a wheel, we look after our partner, home and children and have no licence to change the world, we do whatever we do and feel quite invisible... so how can this thinking and talking about complexity help, change or lead to anything?

At the little world level, the way we manage our lives is up to us. We can choose a complex lifestyle or a simpler lifestyle. By making this choice we can influence our part of the world. Each time an individual chooses to simplify their lives, there is a message to and an impact on, however small, the bigger world. Every time we choose to cut the crap of complexity, we contribute to an incremental movement towards a simpler world.

I am not suggesting we divorce ourselves from the modern world, but that we become a little more critical of it, by turning our mind to the things that add value and those that do not and choosing between these. Cutting complexity from our lives can only come from an acceptance of simplicity. This means a greater level of appreciation and acceptance for what we have, a rejection of greed, waste and excess, and mindful consideration of the impact our lives have on the world (its environment, people, structures).

We need to be prepared to consider that 'now' is 'enough.'

Does this mean we don't look to a future? Does it mean we don't strive to improve our lot? Does it mean we don't have ambition for our children?

No. It does not. But it does mean that if these things do not happen, if we find we do not have a next rung to our ladder, then we can find peace and comfort where we are, and not be tormented by the drive for more, more, more.

The risk we face is that to survive as 'normal' everyday people in the modern world, we bow to the pressure to accept and adopt its complexity. The risk we all face is that this complexity and pressure begins to overtake our lives and our decision-making.

The executive who didn't ever plan to be a workaholic now finds themselves in a job working fourteen hours a day, taking work home every weekend and on call for trouble shooting around the clock. This example applies equally to the successful small-business-person or the surgeon with a successful practice or the teacher who becomes principal. The commonality is the propensity for our complex and pressured work world to dominate and consume our lives. I do not believe that most people plan for this takeover to occur; rather, they lack the insight, awareness and skills to hold back and manage that pressure. They're unable to quarantine work in its own compartment and create other spaces for the rest of life to grow and be rich and positive.

We live in a world where this complexity has driven us to illness and unrest. We are anxious, we are depressed, we are stressed, we burn out. We need help more than any generation before us despite previous famines, economic collapses and world wars. A quarter of our developed-nation populations need psychoactive medications to survive.

Complexity and pressure overload our modern world. Therefore, we need to either accept that discomfort and the wrong that it is, or simply change. What we categorically need to do is make a choice rather than blindly following the new normal. To choose, we must connect to ourselves and our world with insight and active analytic thought. Stop, think, decide, change.

We need to appreciate that complexity is not better than simplicity, that a complicated life is not the hallmark of success and that it's OK to accept a simpler value-driven way.

And when complexity is unavoidable, we must approach it with conscious design and planning rather than fragmented and uncoordinated expansion of relationships and interactions. We must always create behaviours and space that allows us to stand back and observe and measure the effectiveness and efficiency of our complexity.

Any complex system sequesters a few key relationships between structures and processes that are material to the purpose or goal of that system. The challenge is to find these and understand them, and also to find any components that detract from the goal and work to simplify or remove them.

To conclude, I would leave you with these simple thoughts:

A simple solution is always better than a complex one.

Complex systems can be better understood by focusing on a small number of key relationships or processes within them. We need to mitigate complexity by finding the simplicity within it.

Many things have a simple goal – they only become complex when we layer on agendas; the agendas of power, politics, profit and perverse incentives abound in our 'big world'.

The challenge for all of us is to be better than this and, in our own spheres of influence, show that as individuals and as groups we can look for simpler ways to achieve what is required. We can eliminate the stress and pressure of unnecessary complexity. We can cut that crap from our lives and be happier and healthier as individuals, as a society and in our world.

Chapter 20

Friday 19 April 2019

The day was heading to a gentle 20 degrees. The city was beautiful as always, now shaking off its summer coat to bare boughs and branches in many streets and gardens. Harvey had been out early, walking today, not running, allowing himself the luxury of looking and absorbing the tiny things. Sometimes the streets revealed a new feature to the lone walker who was open to contemplate. An architectural feature, a cluster of trees, a park where dogs met to socialise and sniff, a garden painting a picture of late autumn. He wandered on with no particular plan other than to stop somewhere for coffee and escape to the world of everyday life and uncomplicated existence. He'd had his fill of deep thoughts, podcasts and executive manoeuvring for the week and needed space and a seat in the sun. Nothing a week in the South of France wouldn't fix, he thought to himself. That would be nice. Maybe that'd be something to aim for after this next few months disappeared behind him.

The rhythm of the walk was soothing. Through his earphones, the structured peace of Bach's solo cello suites took his mind to a place of stillness and reprieve. Sometimes he could walk for hours on this meditative march around the parks and streets. Walking, watching, listening, absorbing, all and nothing.

Inevitably, after three or four hours, homing and survival instincts brought him back to Noshry, where good coffee, a pan-Asian healthy brunch and all the newspapers were packaged into a cool café with moderately hipster staff who chatted just enough. Their playlist was apparently on-point. It didn't match Harvey's. All the same he enjoyed the mood of the place and the view of the gardens made relaxed escape easy.

Harvey was finishing a second coffee when Elli called.

'Good evening, Harvey,' she said.

'Hi, Elli, good morning, how are you?'

'Just fine,' she replied. 'I was just calling to say thanks for sending 'Simplicity' through today. I've had a look and just had a couple of questions and ideas.'

'Shoot,' said Harvey

'Well, to start I like it a lot. It's more passionate than the others and very thought provoking. The other podcasts have been more inspiring and positive, but this one pushes the listener a bit more. It's more challenging in a way. It's a bit shorter than the others as well – probably will run for 15 minutes or so, which is fine. I don't think we need to make these feel formulaic and mixing them up a bit is good. How would you feel about some real audience questions for five minutes or so at the end? We would edit and produce them, but maybe run a web-based chat room Q&A for some subscribers and use that session to put something together?'

'That sounds good,' replied Harvey. 'I like the idea of some interaction and it may raise some interesting material. Happy to take your lead on that. How are we going with sign-ups this week?'

'Ha-ha!' Elli sounded like she was enjoying herself. 'I thought you would never ask. By yesterday it was just under 68,000 with a rocket. The guys upstairs think this will grow more in the next month then we're beyond counting. I heard the press release went well and

I heard that Jill will be in touch with you about some TV interviews and a couple of radio chat shows next week. I believe we've had an early request about presentation at a conference in Paris in June, but I'll get back to you on that. It looks like we're getting some peaks in uptake on the USA west coast! You should feel immensely proud.'

'I don't know about that. It all feels a little surreal. All I've been doing is writing and recording the stuff then it disappears into the ether to do its thing. I feel weirdly unconnected. In the meantime, life goes on in all its drama here in Sydney.'

Harvey spent a few minutes bringing Elli up to speed on his role change at work. He didn't think there'd be any problem with the podcasts with only two more to go to air, but there had been tension at Queens last week, compounded by the press conference questioning about local issues. Fenland and Hutten had been predictably blunt. Still, usually the hospital hierarchy was happy to surf on the wave of its staff's successes and, either way, Harvey felt no inclination to have them involved at all.

'I think I'll try to get the last script done by the end of next week, Elli. I'm going to get quite busy after that and will need to be on the ball and not thinking so much about the real world outside of work. The local politics and risks of the next two months are not going to be a lot of fun.'

'Are you OK, Harvey?' asked Elli. 'It sounds like things are a bit tough on the ground there and, to be honest, I wondered from the last script if you were unhappy?'

'I'm fine,' replied Harvey. 'I just need to chill a bit and to avoid fallout over the next few weeks. I'll give you a call next week and let you know how 'Integrity' is going… I mean the podcast script, not my job… or maybe I mean both. Lol, talk later.'

Harvey took his time at the café and eventually summoned the energy to drag himself away from the view and comfortable seat in the late morning sun. Before he'd had a chance to settle his bill, and with his head in another place, Harvey almost collided with Joe Crompton as he headed to the counter to pick up some water. He remembered Joe's comments at the regional clinical outcomes meeting and his forgotten pledge to follow up with him. It'd been a busy fortnight and he forgave himself.

'Morning Harvey, you look relaxed?' said Joe.

'Hi Joe,' Harvey said. 'Indeed I am, nothing is quite like a walk, a coffee and a leisurely breakfast on an unplanned day off. I'm starting a project role next week for a couple of months, which will be full-on, so I get a day to chill this week and steel myself.'

'Sounds drastic – what are you doing?'

Harvey explained. 'It's actually looking at a range of governance issues, and the effectiveness of some of the quality management systems at Queens. It seems to be my reward for the questions I have been asking about root cause investigations and other things. Speaking of which – do you remember at the regional outcomes meeting last week I raised that point about central health department reporting of critical incidents and you also tabled similar concerns? Can you share any detail of those?'

'For sure,' said Joe. 'I've been losing sleep over this for the last two months.' An empty footpath table in the sun invited them to stop and talk. Joe was obviously in no hurry and Harvey had all day. The bill could wait. Joe was five or six years older than Harvey, maybe pushing sixty, and had been part of the medical management scene in Sydney for a long time. In the last few years he'd wound back from his previous ICU Director job and worked across the Repat campuses in Clinical Governance and Informatics. Harvey had always respected him as a good thinker and someone with whom it was safe and useful to discuss a new idea or a proposal. He was a little Yoda-ish.

The conversation lasted two pots of tea and more than an hour, and cemented Harvey's concerns. Joe always gave the benefit of any doubt. He avoided paranoid and conspiracy theories about funding and management that most clinicians love to speculate about. He was the Mr Reasonable that our hindsight recommends we should be, so when he told Harvey that he had a handful of issues, which were unresolved and disturbing, Harvey listened.

He started by describing a problem he came upon eight weeks earlier where the Repat hip-replacement infection rate reporting had increased rapidly. A cluster of adverse events or complications like that would normally be reported to the health department and a Root Cause Analysis performed. But the quality manager who made the report was basically told to shelve it by the acting executive manager. Not long after, there had been an instrument left behind in an abdominal procedure. With checklists and procedures this mistake was almost impossible these days. The error was detected before the patient left the OR and the 'solution', that is, reoperating, was completed without obvious harm to the patient. Usually mandatory RCA, this time it was blocked by the same executive on the basis of 'no harm' to the patient. Wrong!

Joe also had a report from the Easton Health psychiatric unit of the suicide of a patient on day leave from the psych ward. Normally, again, this would be a mandatory RCA at health department level. For some reason, the report was shelved, emails disappeared into the cyber junk and the only person with any interest in it remained the quality manager at Easton Health, who'd initiated the report. As it panned out, the Quality Unit at Easton restructured three weeks ago and the said quality manager resigned last week. Joe had known her for at least five years. She was one of the most committed and capable in the district – high integrity and not unreasonably reactive or emotional. The reason for her resignation was not known, but his implication was that the full story would not have been a happy one.

Taking these events and adding in the matters from Queens and the EMS, Harvey and Joe spent fifteen minutes getting them into a more-or-less chronological list, which Harvey typed quickly into his phone:

Hip replacement sepsis cluster, Repat, no RCA

Diabetic death, Queens, no report for RCA

Myocardial Infarction in inappropriately discharged patient, Queens, inaccurate coronial report, no RCA, under investigation by Coroner

Mastenyl dosage issue, EMS, probable Mastenyl substitution and narcotic abuse, no response from EMS

Suicide of mental health patient on leave, Easton Health, RCA suppressed

Surgical instrument retained, Repat, RCA suppressed

Pre-hospital delays, procedural complications, EMS – Asthma death case. No response from EMS, Coroner reviewing

Pre-hospital death rates increasing, EMS, investigating manager 'redeployed'

Quality Unit restructure at Easton, manager resigns.

'What do you think of that little list?' Harvey said.

'Well,' he said, after thinking carefully for a moment, 'I'm not sure that the overall rate of incidents is necessarily alarming. I would bet that in any other three-month period, we'd see a similar number of major incidents across the system or at least in these hospitals. The total in our nine-hospital cluster is usually around seventy-five episodes per year that go to RCA, maybe ninety-five if you count the EMS. So, the rate is not overly alarming. What stands out from the hospitals and health department seems to be a lack of normal process or investigation of these deaths and other system matters. The other worry is the EMS stuff. Because these guys are operating more-or-less solo in a truck, changes in practice and quality of outcomes can be very hard to monitor. You know bias in the reporting and recording is almost guaranteed. There doesn't seem to be any appetite to investigate and when attempts are made by individuals to initiate investigation, they get blocked or diverted. I can't say I've ever seen anything like this before.'

Harvey had a thought. He picked up his phone and opened the contacts, searching for Jemima Reynolds at the health department.

'Hi Jemima, it's Harvey Pearce here. Can I please ask you one quick question without notice?'

'Sure Harvey.' Jemima sounded cheery. 'You're welcome to. I may or may not provide you with an answer, but I will try.'

'Cool. Can you tell me how many investigations have been completed in the last quarter, say January to March?' asked Harvey.

'That should be simple.'

It took her less than a minute to look at the central Root Cause Analysis database and come back to him. 'Harvey, there have been only four completed in that quarter. Is that all you needed?'

'Yes, thanks Jemima.' He rang off and turned back to Joe Crompton.

'Curiouser and curiouser,' said Harvey. 'The total completion rate for investigation of critical incidents and patient-harm episodes for the state in the last quarter is eighty per cent lower than normal.'

Jo replied simply. 'That doesn't happen by chance, Harvey. What are you planning to do about this?'

'I don't know – I was vaguely hoping you might have a solution for me. I guess the bottom line is that someone needs to take this somewhere – health department, government, newspapers, maybe … So far no one seems to be listening,' joked Harvey.

Clearly Jo agreed. 'The real question is: who wants to hear?'

That evening Harvey met up with Jess and Rob at Lina's, a little wine-bar-come-bistro close to the house they shared. It was a favourite Friday night place with smart food and exceptional local and French wines. They were regular enough for the staff to put aside their table in the front corner of the bar. When Harvey arrived, Jess was in deep discussion with their waiter about which Pinot they'd start with. The first bottle of the evening was the serious choice, upon which the orderer would be judged – then who knows where the evening would end after two or sometimes three bottles. Harvey had a strong feeling tonight would be a three-bottler; they had company and there would be plenty to talk about. Not to mention the fact that he was starving and the food here was exceptional.

As he approached the table, Harvey recognised Carol Dubas occupying the usually empty fourth chair. Carol was an international journalist with The Economist and a family friend of Rob's from forever. She had minor local celebrity status and joined their Friday table a few times each year. Carol was a quite beautiful late forty-something single lady, previously married to one of the local health reporters. Harvey had sometimes wondered …

Before he had a chance to sit down, Harvey heard his name from the direction of the bar and looked over to see Todd Fenland perched on a bar stool, intimately close to a considerably younger woman. Clearly Fenland was neither embarrassed nor concerned to have been spotted. On the contrary, he was proud of his company, even flaunting it. Harvey assumed this was due to his inebriation – the level that supplies unshakable self-confidence and parks everyday malice on the shelf labelled bonhomie.

OMG, he thought, no escaping this. He walked over to the bar.

'Hi Todd, fancy seeing you here in the suburbs,' said Harvey.

'My thoughts exactly, Harvey. I admire your taste in wine bars – I haven't been here before, but this place is excellent. Can I introduce you to Shona? Shona this is Harvey Pearce, newest member of our team at work, as well as being super-doc, podcaster and life-saver.'

'Gee thanks, Todd.' Harvey didn't quite know what to say after that introduction. 'Pleased to meet you Shona. Are you guys staying on for dinner? The food here is excellent.'

'No, we're just about to head off for a dinner booking. Is that Jess Goldman you're with?' asked Fenland. 'How's she getting on?'

'Yes, it is,' replied Harvey. 'She's doing very well now. I'm having dinner with Jess and her partner, Rob, and it looks like we also have Carol Dubas to entertain us tonight. I'd better join them. Nice seeing you, catch up Monday.'

'Have a good night Harvey.' Fenland stood to put on his coat and called the waiter to settle his bill.

Harvey joined his friends and apologised for his brief detour. 'So sad that Todd had an engagement and couldn't join us … '

They laughed.

Fenland tipped his hat to Jess as he walked past the front window. Jess groaned. 'That guy is an absolute creep. He makes my skin crawl.'

No sooner had the couple walked away than the waiter approached the table with a bottle of Veuve Clicquot and four glasses. 'Complements of Mr Fenland I believe,' she said. The four looked at each other, dumbfounded.

Rob was the first to recover. 'Crawling skin or not, I, for one, am happy. Cheers!'

As the laughter died down, Harvey felt better than he had all week, looking forward to a little excess and a long evening with his friends.

―᠊ᡟ᠊ᡟ᠊ᡟ᠊―

Fenland had driven off, barely clearing the curb before hitting his speed dial to Hutten.

'Yes, I'm sure it was Dubas,' he said, 'with Goldman and some other guy.'

'I'm not sure what to make of that,' replied Hutten. 'She's not exactly on the local tabloid hustings, but who knows?'

Hutten ended the call, and about the same time as the foursome toasted Fenland with a glass of Veuve, he hit the send button on a text to Minister Henderson.

―᠊ᡟ᠊ᡟ᠊ᡟ᠊―

The evening passed quickly. Harvey managed some lame flirting with Carol. Their eye contact suggested to him that a phone call next week might be sensible. She left by 10.30pm, after excusing herself because of an early flight to New York. Rob saw her to a cab at the front door. When he returned to the table, he told Harvey that if he didn't get in contact with Carol, he would irrevocably classify him as a complete fool. Harvey could say nothing. Instead, he changed the subject.

Chapter 21

Lina's

'You know I caught up with Joe Crompton today,' he said, with the directness that his share of the Champagne and Pinot afforded. 'We'd both raised concerns about the investigation of critical incidents recently so sat down and pooled our knowledge. As it turns out, Joe had some intelligence from Easton Health that amounted to more of the same. We now have a list involving three hospitals plus the EMS and God knows how many patients. We have evidence of systematic under-reporting and cover-up of patient harm. There is a clear picture of at least a handful of known deaths. Joe's been around a long time and he's never come across such a comprehensive cluster of hush-ups. It's all shaping into something very ugly and, for some people, very deadly.'

Rob had started into his Tarte Tatin but put his fork down. 'Harvey, don't close your book yet. I've been sniffing about also and there's more to add to your list. Word has it that last month there was a paramedic death from Mastenyl. No one seems to know if it was deliberate or accidental, but the source is reliable. There's categorically an in-house investigation going on and the assumption is that both cops and government are aware, but no one is saying anything. The union hasn't been engaged and the guys on the ground haven't received any useful communication, so you can imagine what the rumour mill is doing. This is likely to go ballistic when the word gets out, and I would imagine it'll be soon.'

Harvey had pulled out his phone and added some notes to the list.

'I see you're being literal about having a list,' said Jess. 'You know there is more, so keep typing.' She said looking over at Rob suggesting it was his turn to add to the pile.

'What do you mean?' asked Harvey.

Unlike him, Rob hesitated for a moment. Harvey wondered what this was going to be. The material they had already was damning and disgraceful. What could be worse?

Rob began. 'Harvey, I was at the incident review meeting last week, and there was a case presented of procedural awareness that came to us through a patient complaint. Two months ago, the EMS sedated and intubated a young girl, teenager, with asthma. It turned out that the Mastenyl used for her sedation was mainly water … as per our known dilution scenario. As is usual, she was paralysed to be intubated and put on to the ventilator and so, courtesy of the tampered Mastenyl, was fully awake for the entire procedure. She was paralysed but aware, heard everything and later even recounted what the paramedics had said in their handover at the hospital. Can you imagine the terror?' Rob looked physically pained and pushed his dessert well away.

'This is bad enough, but it gets worse. The report comes from the family to our complaints unit and goes for investigation and through the usual review. It ends up tabled at the meeting as a level-two incident. Because of its classification as a level two or 'possible patient harm' incident rather than a level one or 'death or definite serious patient harm' it goes no further. It avoids Root Cause Analysis and health department reporting, which is mandatory for all level one incidents. At this point in the meeting, I was getting agitated and asked the chair if they thought it reasonable to assume patient harm in this case? Wouldn't we be right to assume that an episode like this will cause at least a level of psychological harm, if not a major PTSD?

In response I was treated to a pile of BS about the fact that Sydney EMS almost never receive information back from hospitals about patient outcomes, our databases are not linked, and we cannot obtain information from the hospitals about outcomes because of privacy legislation. If harm isn't 100 percent proven then it is 'deemed' not to have happened.

Therefore, apparently, we can rarely if ever be aware of a true level-one outcome and therefore almost never be required to investigate systematic harm issues or need to report these incidents to the department. Somehow, just somehow, I don't believe that this game the EMS is playing is right.'

Rob leant forward into the table and lowered his voice.

'Harvey, bottom line is that this is one fucked-up system that no one is motivated to fix.'

Harvey put down his phone, having added three points to his list:

Paramedic death from stolen Mastenyl

Patient awareness episode related to use of tampered Mastenyl

EMS lack of access to routine hospital patient follow-up information resulting in apparent ignorance of poor outcomes.

They were all aware that the question they faced was 'what to do now?' Harvey felt a heaviness, both uncomfortable and real. He saw at once that his friends were also affected. Jess echoed his inner question.

'So, what now?' she said. 'We know there's a combination of things happening here. On one hand we have what looks like increased frequency of patient harm and on the other we know that the system is hampering review of critical failures. The risk to patients and to our colleagues is huge.'

Rob sighed. 'And behind this we have something going on, which is shutting down reporting and throwing a fire blanket over the lot.'

'We can't be the only ones who've worked this out,' said Harvey. 'The silence on reporting and escalation of this is bizarre. It would take a lot of pressure to put up the shutters in health department channels, and the risks attached to that are massive. It'd also be impossible to support this fiasco long-term, so the idea of this being a political short-term fix makes a lot of sense. It also means there's likely to be organised and potent resistance to any attempt to shine a light on the issue.'

'I think we need to be careful.' Rob was showing a degree of uncharacteristic reservation. 'The idea that there are others who've reached these conclusions will be correct. Maybe this is a time for strength in numbers, not lonesome warriors.'

Both Harvey and Jess agreed. Harvey went on to explain to Rob and Jess about his conversations with Hutten and Fenland over the last week and his change in role at Queens.

'I wouldn't mind looking at this from the lofty heights of the exec floor at Queens before we lock in on next steps,' said Harvey. 'If there is a back story here that involves the Health Minister and a need to keep a lid on pre-election bad press, the connections might all become a bit more … ' Harvey stopped. Seconds passed as he thought through the scenario that had just dawned on him. He looked up at Jess and Rob, both sitting patiently, poised on his next words.

'I think I know what's happening. OK, this government is on a knife's edge with the election looming quickly. To be voted out of office, they only need a swing against them of perhaps two per cent and they're now campaigning madly on the back of connected construction industry dollars. This collection of incidents would probably be enough to fuel a press action that could topple them. Rob, let's assume your information is correct about dirty election funds and a move for the Health Minister to Business and Planning, and that Hutten's wife picks up the Health Ministry. Wouldn't it be cool if in her first few months in office, she was able to solve a historic and serious problem in the health system? She could show the world what a decisive and effective politician she'd become. Wouldn't it be cool if there was some dummy called Harvey, for instance, who they appointed to do a review and report on all this after the election was over, and which would provide her with a phenomenal career-rocketing opportunity.' He paused another moment to get the storyline right.

'I think my job over the next few months is to uncover what Fenland and Hutten and our soon-to-be Health Minister Chantier already know and present that to them on a plate at a time that suits their plan. The timing of my so-called promotion is no accident. They would understand that while the review is going on, irritation and reaction settles for a while, and the press will concentrate on other things. Having someone do this who has a recent and high-profile social-media presence in the life-integrity space will lend kudos to the report and eventual publicity.

'The government avoids a pre-election scud, Chantier becomes a hero, Hutten is left sitting in a position of great favour, and I am a tool,' finished Harvey. He knew he was right.

Jess added quietly, 'And in the meantime another handful of people die or suffer because the timing to fix this politically sensitive issue is not quite convenient … '

'I know what you're saying, Jess,' replied Harvey, 'but maybe this new position will let me get some solid information on what's behind all this. If I can do that quickly then maybe we can put a stop to all this craziness for good.'

'I pretty much agree Harvey, but I think your review is just going to describe the problem we already know about, just on a larger scale. I'd be very surprised if there will be any smoking guns to be found or anything that will take it back to the pollies.' Jess finished the remainder of her Pinot and Rob poured another half glass. She said 'thanks' with her eyes.

They finished their last drinks and the trio paid up and left Lina's. Harvey walking slowly over to a cab while Jess and Rob wandered home, arms around each other, bracing against a cool breeze. Winter was on the way.

There was a lot to think about. They sat at home a short while later, quietly digesting the evening and sipping a late-night Scotch on the rocks.

'I'm more than a bit worried about Harvey,' said Rob.

'I know,' said Jess. 'And I feel like a whimp taking leave right now. Having someone else around to watch his back wouldn't go astray.'

'Alex is there, and remember, your priority is staying well,' he said tenderly.

Although Rob said nothing directly, Jess couldn't help herself from thinking about her struggle with burnout and then back to 2014, Guinea and Medicin Sans Frontieres. That'd been a rough deployment, which left her with scars. She topped up their Scotch and closed her mind to the past.

Curled up on the couch together, they were unable to solve any more of the world's problems but found themselves in a heady closeness. The combination inevitably drew them completely together.

Jess woke at 2am, still on the couch and naked underneath a mohair blanket that Rob had placed over her before he had taken himself to bed. She could sleep anywhere and, after Scotch and lovemaking, a soft couch and sumptuous blanket felt just fine.

But now she was awake and some of her early thoughts returned. She opened her iPad in search of distraction and starting flicking through old photos. Whether from Rob's comment or her own subconscious navigator, she found herself in an album from 2014 titled 'Guinea'. It was the beginning of her PTSD and probably the start of her current issues with work.

Her deployment through ASIO had been made to look like a secondment from AUSMAT to Medicins Sans Frontier, ostensibly to help in provision of emergency services in the Ebola outbreak in Guinea. There was much more to her placement than that, and she spent a difficult six months avoiding risks posed by both Ebola and Russians. The former was potentially life threatening, but the latter were more exasperating. Her work amounted to very little in the end; however, at the time there was much political interest in Russian influence in West Africa, including games they were believed to be playing in local politics, arms distribution, the mining sector and, just maybe, in weapons-level virology. Many thought the outbreak was anything but a 'natural' public health emergency, and that it was predictable that one autocracy or other would one day unleash a bio-catastrophe on the world – maybe Ebola, maybe SARS, maybe something else.

She managed to bring home a sub-clinical malarial infection, the beginnings of PTSD and little useful intelligence, and decided soon after to part ways with her government employers and return to emergency medicine.

The next year had been difficult between recovery and readjustment, but with some help she had largely mended and moved on. The photos took her back to that period with a kind of numb detachment, but the guilt she had in walking away made her stop.

She'd go back to work and cancel her leave. She'd hang in with Harvey, cover the department for him while he was on secondment to the exec role, and do whatever she could to help him out. He had a lot stacked up against him and this was the least she could do.

It was getting cold so she took herself off to bed.

When she awoke next morning, Jess remembered to send Harvey a quick SMS to let him know she was cancelling her leave and would be at work on Monday. His reply.

<Cheers, Grateful! You can cover my roster – day shifts only for the next month. Chat later. HP>

She was happy with her decision.

Chapter 22

Fortnight of 22 April 2019

Harvey found himself trying to take a pragmatic approach over the following fortnight. He told himself he could live with the delay of another two months or so. Then he'd have a completed report, drawing on material from other health services and the EMS and developed by a professional team. He wondered if it'd carry more weight than the list of anecdotes he'd started with. At any rate it was realistic to assume that a government on the edge of an election was not going to engage with this topic until after the poll. It made sense to wait.

If he was wrong, and there was no sinister conspiracy being directed by Fenland, Hutten and their political connections, then waiting was simply delaying a solution, delaying removal of huge risks to many patients.

If he was correct and the condescension of these political players was as pitiless as it seemed, then the incidental wreckage of a few lives or a system of health safety may not matter to them at all. This harm would continue until the machination was exposed.

But what made sense did not equal what he felt. He thought about the motivations of the low-life playing this game. How desperate could you be to succeed? How indifferent could you be to the suffering of other people? Would you stop for a second and think about the 12-year-old girl in the ED, screaming with pain from her burns? Would you spend some quiet time thinking about the families left behind? The wife and children of the young man with heart disease who didn't need to die; the partner of the paramedic who was the victim of a system that wouldn't protect him from himself? Would you think about the staff who worked in your hospitals then quit a decade before their use-by date because you chose to starve their systems of funding and integrity and safety… until they burnt out?

Or would you see none of these, because you didn't care to look?

――

By the time Hutten's review project reached Wednesday of week two, Harvey knew that a six-to-eight-week timeframe would be unnecessary. His impatience would not last that long. And, at the rate information was coming in, there would be no need.

For the first week he spoke with clinical governance leaders from all of the regional health services and gathered case after case for review. For each organisation he mapped out the health of their clinical governance systems and processes, looking for strengths and weaknesses. The consistency of their methods was not surprising. Each typically composed a framework or philosophy supported by documentation of policy and systems of education. Processes of clinical quality, outcome measurement and systems for involvement of practitioners, community, patients and partners were all present. The architecture of the system was right.

However, repetitive stories of incidents, and recurring episodes of process failure appeared from many directions, as did unexplainable staff movements, retirements and reassignments of people who'd been working in the quality and safety space for years. Chronic themes of defensive, vague interactions with the EMS that never reached resolution were repeated.

His small team consisted of an administrative assistant and two project workers. One, Naomi Symson, was an intern solicitor with an interest in health law and the other Terry Frankes, was an earnest master's student in health management. Both were bright and energetic. Both were naïve enough to be untainted in their approach. Harvey kept his private theories to himself; he wanted their work to be objective, not influenced by his cynicism or prejudice.

He fed them a method and then handed them case after case to review, their task to draw conclusions about the processes applied, the recommendations reached, the compliance with policy and the actions taken to avoid future harm. Each case involved four-to-six-hours' work and by the middle of the second week they presented him with seventeen completed reviews. There were another fourteen cases to look at and four focus groups to run.

By the time he'd read their comments on Wednesday evening, Harvey knew his theories were realistic and painfully accurate. Although Naomi and Terry had not tied all the material together or been able to explain a systematic mechanism for all the problems, the themes were there. Cover-up, disrupt, delay. Incidents like the patients who died could be made to temporarily disappear, perhaps to reappear when they could be managed with less fallout in the future. Even better, they'd be filed away and forgotten.

Harvey felt vindicated, but also, and perhaps incongruously he felt lower than ever before. By Thursday 2 May he was close to resignation and took the day off to clear his mind and resolve what he could.

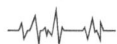

On Friday 3 May 2019 Harvey started his day in the usual way with coffee and newspapers. This Thursday his coffee sat untouched. The front page of the Sydney Morning Herald had one large photo and a single banner. The photograph was a dramatic black and white grainy shot of a busy ambulance bay at an unrecognisable hospital. The banner simply said Healthcare in Crisis.

Opening to the first double spread revealed three articles and a group of photographs and illustrations. Crowded emergency department corridors, a sad family group with no father, a paramedic leaning exhausted or distressed against his ambulance, a table of data, an annotated graph. Harvey knew what he was about to read …

The Health Minister has declined to comment about reports of serious incidents, cover-ups, patient injury and deaths occurring across our health system …

… Reliable sources have informed the Sydney Morning Herald that the government has acted to actively suppress investigation of major critical incidents in hospitals across the state…

… Sources who prefer to remain anonymous have advised that the EMS in greater Sydney is in crisis after multiple recent narcotic overdoses in paramedics. It is alleged that widespread theft of narcotics from ambulance stock has been occurring. It is believed that paramedics are abusing stolen drugs and selling narcotics …

… Hospital staff have advised that numerous episodes of patient injury and deaths in recent months have been covered up and that normal reporting and investigation systems have been suppressed …

… Hospital crowding and under staffing have reached peak levels due to budget constraint. At the same time, hundreds of thousands of dollars have been earmarked for major health construction work …

... It is believed that the Coroner's office is currently investigating up to ten suspicious deaths related to episodes of care in either ambulance or hospital. Family describe how a husband and father was sent home from the hospital emergency department to die alone from coronary disease.

... Confidential sources have revealed that death rates due to complications of paramedic procedures have skyrocketed. The same sources describe disturbing increases in delays to transport of patients from the scene of injury or accident to nearby emergency departments.

... Delays and congestion in hospital emergency departments result in unprecedented patient discomfort and harm. Patients spend hours lying on trolleys in corridors with little or no care.

... Family claim that a child with serious burns pain received no relief from EMS staff due to tampering with ambulance drugs.

... Hospital quality and safety manager resigns.

... Hospital staff turnover and burnout hits peak rates.

... Pre-election health crisis cover-ups beyond the pale ... Calls for the resignation of the Health Minister Henderson ...

... Opposition party has called for an urgent Royal Commission; however, the seriousness of the accusations in this matter may trigger direct referral to the Public Prosecutor ...

Most of the pieces were written by Thomas Gallant. Harvey didn't know Thomas well but had met him on a couple of social occasions when he was still married to Carol Dubas. He'd been a health journalist for years and was known for careful research and balanced pieces, some of which had reached national circulation.

The coverage extended to almost three pages in all and included several cases that Harvey was aware of. There were others he hadn't come across, such as references to behaviours, factions and bullying inside the EMS. The articles hinted at, but stayed short of, explicit accusations of motive and mechanisms for the cover-ups. In references to 'union and industry' and 'political drivers' there was enough to suggest the reporters knew much more but were holding back.

Harvey surprised himself with his lack of reaction. Ten years ago, he would have been punching the air by now. Maybe it was age and maturity, maybe it was tiredness, maybe it was the realisation that this leaked truth was the story of avoidable misery and hurt for dozens of individuals and their families. This was a story of wasted labour and effort, wasted commitment from healthcare staff around the state, wasted dedication to their patients and a system of caring and healing.

He was pleased because the callous motivations of the orchestrators could now be uncovered. Open rage, shame and resentment would be everywhere. The reactions he'd needed to suppress would be expressed by many in the business. The game he'd been forced to play and the placation he'd endured could be dispensed with. People would ask why it took the press to uncover this disaster, why there'd been no action, why no one had realised or spoken up. They'd see failure in the actions of the Harveys and Joe Cromptons and others who'd walked away or said nothing about their suspicions, because they weren't strong enough to stand up for what they'd seen. Compromised by the political game which enveloped them.

The work that he and Naomi and Terry and others had done would contribute to inquiries and would not be wasted.

Harvey made himself another coffee and found his cigarettes in a draw he used to hide them. He took both onto his terrace and sat there for just a few minutes before he came in, showered, dressed, grabbed a portable hard disk from his desk and walked down to Queens.

The walk through the park and gardens was slow and deliberate and gave Harvey time to think. Before the day progressed, he wanted to secure his files and the records of his team's case reviews and actions. He also wanted to make sure he had copies of emails and notes. There was little doubt that blame-shifting would be a strategy employed in any defence of Gallant's claims, and Harvey wanted the truth preserved.

When Naomi and Terry arrived at the office, Harvey was at his desk with USB disk whirring beside his computer. Together they came into his office, clear that today would bring some interesting conversations but unsure of what this would mean for the work they'd completed so far.

'So, what do you make of this morning's article?' Harvey said.

Terry kicked off. 'It certainly looks like someone's been reading our mail. Harvey, Naomi and I met over a coffee this morning before we came up and went through the material in the newspaper. Each of the cases referenced in the articles is on our files and the little published detail matches what we've found. We do have quite a few cases that are not referred to and the detail we have on the level of investigation and actions taken or, more importantly, not taken, is not really covered by Gallant.'

Naomi added, 'If Gallant had access to our files, he would've had quite a bit more fuel for this fire. Maybe he's planning to release more over time, but I would be surprised. The article looks to be aiming to blow the lid off the issue and I think if he had more, he'd have used it.'

'Who knows?' replied Harvey. 'There're two things I've learnt from dealing with the press in the last twenty-five years: never try to understand the motives of a newspaper and never trust a journalist. Although I'm excited about seeing this all over the news, there's now a real risk that our work will stall for some time. Now, there are a few things we need to cover off this morning before the world explodes, and I expect it will.

The first is: have we had a security breach?

I don't think we have, but it can be difficult to be sure. I've spoken with the IT security desk and they haven't found anything suspicious. Can I assume that neither of you have lost a computer or a USB drive or had anyone access to your machines?'

Both Terry and Naomi looked at him with innocent alarm. It clearly had not occurred to them that they would be considered responsible for the information leak or that there may have been a hack of their files.

'No,' replied Naomi. 'I haven't taken my computer out of the office in the last two weeks.'

'I have,' Terry said, 'but there's no chance anyone has had access to it and I don't keep work stuff on portable disks.' He was looking at Harvey's external drive, blinking away on the desk.

'Well spotted,' said Harvey. 'As of now I am making copies of all our file notes and downloading our mail archives. The last thing we need is for these files to go missing.' He frowned. 'The other thing I need to ask you is whether you've had any conversations about this material with the press or anyone who could have leaked to them?'

Harvey didn't think for a moment that either would have been the source, and both denied responsibility. Soon he was satisfied that none of the information had come from them.

'OK,' he said, 'let's just see where this goes today. Last night I read the summaries you gave me and I made a few notes, tracked in the files. What I would like you to do is review those comments, fill in gaps where you can, then start cataloguing and cross-referencing common themes. Tidy up any loose ends you can. That'll keep us busy this week and we can see where we go after that.'

Harvey completed his file backup – not something the IT security policy would recommend. Keeping a backup disk off the main servers was probably not above-board, but he wasn't about to ask anyone for advice. He wondered if the fact that he was downloading all this material and email archives would leave a trail. Either way, it was done now.

The morning dragged on and he called Todd Fenland's administrative assistant to arrange a time to talk with him. He assumed the conversations would already be happening on the eighth floor. By mid-morning he'd not heard anything and was mildly concerned, so when the knock at his door announced a visit from the CEO, Harvey was startled.

Hutten entered the room, closing the door behind him. The expression on his face was cold and non-committal. Harvey suspected there was anger not far below the surface.

'Harvey, I am going to get straight to the point – what do you know about the material in the Sydney Morning Herald this morning?' said Hutten.

'Probably about the same as you,' replied Harvey. 'I've discussed this with our staff already and am confident the material didn't come from them. We have significantly more material than was published, with quite a lot more detail about let's call it 'systematic inaction', which I'm sure Gallant would have gone to town on if he'd had it. I've checked with IT and they're not aware of any system penetration or hacking. But I would think, based on the work we've completed so far, that Gallant's sources and material are fully accurate.'

Hutten remained standing, his hands gripping the back of the chair in front of Harvey's desk.

'I've had a call from the health department, in fact about ten calls. They're obviously aware that you have been probing this space for months. They're also worried about the source and that makes me extremely worried.'

The feeling in the pit of Harvey's stomach was unmistakeable. He was in the crosshairs and unsure which way to turn. Defence. Avoidance. Truth?

'I'm sure they are worried.' Harvey adopted his most measured tone. 'I think we're all worried about these issues. There are a range of reasons why different people are worried, and some have more at risk than others. So, I think we need to be careful about how we react and what we say. Roger, there's been noise on the ground out there for months from the unions, EMS, other hospitals, even the health department. The information that Gallant has is correct, but, in my view, it could have come from any number of sources.'

'Maybe,' said Hutten, 'but not all of those sources have been talking across the whole health system, and not all of those sources fraternise with journalists.' Hutten's face became less cold and more clearly agitated as he leaned forward in his chair and dropped his voice. 'Harvey, there are people who stand to suffer a lot as a result of this. I don't think I believe you or swallow your 'this could have been anyone talking' crap ... Todd Fenland saw you last week drinking with Carol Dubas and a couple of your chums. Dubas' connection to Gallant may be history, but I doubt it's dead. If there's a good story involved, I'd guarantee they're still in each other's contact lists.'

'You're on the wrong track, Roger.' To be honest, Harvey was a bit miffed at the accusation. If he wanted to leak information, he'd be a bit more subtle than that. 'Carol, Jess, Rob and I are old friends, and Carol keeps her work out of our social space.'

'Sure, and journalists protect their sources.' Hutten paused. 'You know what, Harvey? I don't think this is going to work out so well ... The best thing is for you to fuck off out of here.' His agitation then gave way to an expression as empty as possible. His words and his face seemed disconnected, but the message was clear. 'I want you gone in half an hour and your flunkies out there can report to

Todd Fenland. I'll let you know what action we're going to take. But Harvey – you know what – I don't see a future for you with this organisation.'

Harvey was staggered. 'This is total bullshit, Roger. There is no evidence that anyone here has leaked anything to the press and what you've said is extremely fucking unreasonable. Is there more to this than I am aware of? Is there a personal agenda or do you have a stake in this?' Harvey knew he was throwing fuel on the fire.

Hutten looked Harvey full in the face with anger and hate. He was thinking, but all he came up with was, 'Fuck off, you self-righteous prick.'

For Harvey that said it all.

'Roger I'm sure you're aware of the information floating around about government and management suppression of incident reporting and safety, and I assume you have heard the rumours about construction money and the election campaign – I guess your wife will have filled you in on that … I don't think this is a smart time to be shutting down an established investigation into this issue. Have you given any thought to the implications of what you're doing?'

Hutten stood up silently and moved to the door, turning as he placed his hand on the knob. 'Goodbye Harvey'.

Chapter 23

Friday Afternoon, 3 May 2019

Harvey walked into Lamaro's Bar with the thought of drowning his sorrows and immediately felt like a living cliché. Still, it was a nice enough place to escape to. He made himself comfortable planning some lunch and a glass or two, but as the afternoon progressed so did the plan …

He had left the office after talking with Terry and Naomi. He explained as much as possible to them, and although he was exasperated, he reassured them as best he could. Their work would continue in some form and, at worst, they'd be redeployed to their home departments. The review would be scuttled, as a larger central investigation was likely to emerge from the breaking news. He kept political connections and election funding out of the conversation, and thanked them for their work.

The TV in the corner of the bar was playing interviews from local politicians on its endless news cycle. Jane Chantier was trying to placate the reporters with unconvincing sound bites. Chantier was an over-groomed woman whose sole facial expression of superiority and privilege was exactly the opposite of what the government needed at this moment. Her handling of a press conference in the early afternoon was poor – her responses stalling after the announcement that her department would initiate a formal inquiry.

No mention of the patients and families hurt, no reference to the paramedics and health service staff caught up in this, no apologies.

The least she could have done was express some concern for all these people, perhaps a little 'sorry', perhaps a connection to the humanity in all this. That wasn't Jane. And it didn't surprise Harvey that by mid-afternoon, the government press office had packed her into a back room somewhere and rolled out the Health Minister. At least her performance was more polished, but it was unlikely that the public would be instantly reassured on this score. The press would stay on this for weeks.

Harvey's phone had been running hot for most of the day. He was now at the point of letting calls go through to message bank, which simply led to a pile of SMS messages that he'd answer another time.

He noticed one from Rob, which he read straight up.

<Yo Harvey, who dropped the bomb? Heading in for late shift now - catch-up and hit the court tomorrow morning??>.

Harvey couldn't help a half smile to himself and replied:

<Was going to make the same observation, pal. Shit hits fan! No probs. OK for about nine tomorrow but ? wastage at Lamaro's>.

There was another from Elli Clemence.

<Hi Harvey, can you call, just chasing 'integrity', lol E>.

To which he replied,

<Sorry E, world imploding here, check Sydney Morning Herald online, will send you draft now. TTYL Harvey>.

He opened Dropbox and sent the file. It wasn't quite finished, but it would do for the time being.

A little later, about 3.30pm, Harvey received a call from Tom Gallant. He didn't recognise the mobile number and picked up. Mistake. 'In light of recent developments,' Gallant said he 'was looking for an official comment from Queens Hospital, could Harvey help out?'

Yeah sure, thought Harvey.

Harvey was on his third beer and, having added two Jamesons to break up the pattern, thought it was undoubtedly not the right time for an interview or comment, and so directed Gallant to the Queens switchboard, suggesting he talk with Todd Fenland.

The call Harvey made to Fenland five minutes later reinforced his view of the guy and, as he picked up, Harvey wondered why he was bothering to give him a heads up.

'Todd, it's Harvey here, I am just calling to let you know that I've had a call from Thomas Gallant, who is after comment from the hospital about the review. I've pointed him in your direction. To be honest I couldn't be stuffed talking to him, although the temptation to blow this whole thing open was truly fucking profound.'

Fenland didn't appreciate being told. 'I suspect you've already done way too much talking to Gallant. If I were you, I'd shelve the lip – you'd be well advised to pull your head in.'

'Well, thanks for that advice, Todd.' Harvey hoped he wasn't slurring. 'But right now, I'm preoccupied with a little relaxation at Lamaro's, where I'm chilling and watching your games go to shit on the TV.'

What the hell? I wonder why these arseholes are so convinced I'm Gallant's source. With our review grinding on through the upper floors at Queens, nothing would've come out till after the election. Maybe in the end, we would've achieved what we needed to. But now, you could bet there'll be a massive government enquiry, all the health services'll hire consultants to do external impartial reviews, the cops'll be onto the Mastenyl debacle and that'll take forever to get to the bottom of. The Coroner might move it all along a bit faster, but their machine's wheels turn slowly, too. In a year we may get a resolution and it'll take another year for a remedy. In the meantime, what happens? Nothing?

If I were them, I would have put my money on a leak from the EMS. There can't be many people outside that service who know about the issues there, not really. Coroners maybe? They don't leak as a rule but …

Hardly worth trying to guess. The EMS governance guys would know what's been happening in hospitals and with investigations and they must be across their own death and complication rates. Fact is I seem to be wearing it for everybody. By the time the truth comes out, the damage will be done. Hutten and Fenland will smear me as well as they can, and there's not much I can do about it.

Truth may prevail, but when? And at what cost? Can I be bothered or is this just one hassle too many? I'm tired, so tired. This is exhausting, frustrating bullshit that is just sapping me stupid. Why so unmanageable? I've confronted it and look where that's got me – but what was the option?

Has this just made everything too complicated? Maybe time to get out of this business, to cut the crap. Hah, the irony …

Is that even real? Cut the crap. How precious, how contrived, how pretentious to run around telling the world to cut the crap. What a wanker. Does that make me hollow, just part of this whole mess of being? I don't know, I really don't know what the next step should be.

Resign? Move on? Just cut and run and leave this catastrophe behind?

Not really an option, not my style. Better to hang in and get ready for a rough ride – but how to avoid being the scapegoat?

Need a plan. A good plan. Need a strategy. But not now. Now is escape, plan later ... or not ... whatever.

It was empty-glass o'clock, so time for another trip to the bar where he perched for a while, having followed an Irish theme, migrated from Jameson's to Redbreast via Guinness, and developed his relationship with the bar tender a little further. An hour later, Harvey and the afternoon were mostly written off, and the counsellor behind the bar suggested coffee, which was good advice. Harvey made his way back to the armchair he'd been using earlier and drank a glass of water while he waited for the black coffee to arrive.

Then Harvey saw him coming. What started as a silhouette at the backlit doorway evolved into a face he didn't want to see. The face stopped, looked around and spotted Harvey.

'WTF?' groaned Harvey. 'What is he doing here?'

Todd Fenland sat down in the chair opposite.

'I thought you'd still be here, Harvey. You're not picking up calls? Drinking alone is said to be pathological you know.'

'There's a lot of pathology in the world.' Harvey heard the coffee machine start up.

'Have you got any idea how much you've pissed people off?'

'What people?' Harvey said.

'Important people.' Fenland looked like he needed a drink. 'I don't think you have any idea how much shit this has stirred up. The impact of this on the government, ministers and a whole lot of invested parties is way beyond your understanding. You know, you would have got there in the end if you'd let things run their course, but instead you wanted to bash down the door, not knock and wait. The only thing worse than a zealot is one who doesn't understand the game.'

Harvey wondered if he should buy the man a drink and then leave. 'Park it, I've had enough of all that shit for one day and you've got it all wrong. Quite frankly, I don't give a toss what Hutten and Mrs Fucking Hutten and the Health Minister and all their heavy political and construction buddies and fucking benefactors think.'

The coffee arrived. Harvey knocked it back while they talked around in circles for the next fifteen minutes until the newcomer suggested to Harvey that he may as well drink to his demise. He went to the bar and came back with a pair of Rusty Nails. Harvey agreed that was a fitting way to end an afternoon at Lamaro's and he was not about to say no to one-for-the-road.

Fenland sank into the other armchair. Harvey thought he looked drained – and a bit pathetic. He didn't have much to say but did manage to ask Harvey what his plans were for his time off.

Harvey didn't have a clue.

Then Fenland said 'I'm heading home. I can drop you off at your place on the way.' Maybe he wasn't a total arsehole.

Harvey went over to the bar on the way out and left a twenty. He was tired, very tired, and his words made no sense as he thanked the barman for a forgettable afternoon.

Chapter 24

The next morning, Rob found Harvey's body.

The following week was a blur. He and Jess took a couple of days and headed to the Blue Mountains to hide from the world. But there was no hiding their misery and the prospect of Harvey's funeral hung over them.

On the second day Rob started working on a eulogy. He hated the word and he hated the thought, and before he completed the first line he dissolved in a flood of tears that just came from nowhere.

The week didn't get any better for either of them, but somehow they fronted for work on Wednesday. By then, word had circulated and of course, no one was saying anything.

Friday 10 May 2019

After the service, many of those who had attended Harvey's funeral retreated to Lamaro's. Rob opened proceedings by making a toast to Harvey. It was brief and he apologised for the morbid twist - sending Harvey off from the scene of his last stand, but Rob explained that the irony of this would have suited Harvey perfectly.

The turnout was predictably impressive. Elli Clemence had flown in from Germany, and there were several out-of-towners from Harvey's past. Elli had approached Rob and asked him about Harvey's family – to which he had replied and pointed out Charlotte. A little later, Elli introduced herself to Harvey's sister, and sat with her for a while. 'Charlotte, I know this is a grim time, but I just want to pass on my respects. I'm Elli Clemence, Harvey's producer for his podcast work. I'm not sure how much you knew about Harvey's recent podcasting, but he'd become quite the international success. He has thousands of followers, and even now that he's gone, I think there'll be many people accessing his podcasts as new subscribers in the future. What he had to say will continue to resonate with people.'

Charlotte was younger than Harvey, a lawyer in Melbourne, and she sat with her two boys, mid teens, Elli thought. She replied, 'Thank you so much, Elli. Harvey had spoken of you, and of his amusement with the podcasting world. It's wonderful to think of it as a meaningful legacy, I guess.'

'I agree,' said Elli. 'Would you be OK if I came and talked with you in a week or two? You know Harvey sent me an almost-complete draft of what was to be the final podcast in this series, and I would like to have someone record it and get it posted. It seems fitting.'

'Yes, it does.' said Charlotte.

—⋎⋏⋎—

Rob and Jess escaped from the larger group and took up a quiet position at the corner of the bar. The barman poured their drinks and lingered for just a moment then stopped and turned toward Jess and Rob. 'You know, I was working here that last time Harvey came in. He was a good guy and didn't usually drink that much. He tipped well and was a polite drunk on that last occasion.' He smiled. 'It's hard to believe is all I've got to say.'

'Thanks,' said Rob. 'Yes, it is hard to believe.' He looked at Jess. She was about to cry again. Rob raised his glass to the barman who wandered off.

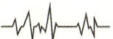

The afternoon was slowing. People started to drift away. The crowd distilled down to a hard core of closer friends and work mates. The bosses and dignitaries had left, and Charlotte and her boys had gone. Rob was standing at the corner of the bar and Jess had gone off to the rest rooms, when Phil Vancleef came over to speak with him.

'Hey Rob,' he said.

'Phil, howdy. How are you travelling?'

'Yeah, I'm travelling OK, I suppose. You know, despite working at the Coroner's office and being in the death business, I don't think it gets any easier to deal with death when it's in your own world like this.'

'I know what you mean,' said Rob.

Phil finished what was left of the Jameson's in his glass. 'Rob, can I ask you something about Harvey?'

'Sure, just as long as we don't speak ill of the dead.' Rob knew it was a weak joke, but it was the best he could do.

'This is a bit left-field, Rob, but did you ever know Harvey to be a K user?'

'No way, Phil. Harvey was a straight fine-wine and good spirits guy, give or take the odd beer. He wouldn't even touch a joint.' He paused. 'That doesn't sound like a question a Coroner would – or should – ask for no reason.'

'No, it's not,' said Phil. 'Something weird came back from our lab late yesterday. It was an amended report on Harvey's Tox screen. In addition to the Propofol that was obviously at the scene, the lab detected an almost imperceptible trace of Ketamine. I mean, the sort of level you might see with contamination of a specimen or maybe where the drug was all but fully metabolised and excreted at the time the sample was collected. In this case, death.'

'I don't get it.' Rob was getting edgy. 'There's no chance in hell that Harvey would take K and, anyway, why would he need to? There was enough Propofol there to kill Michael Jackson twice! And we only found Propofol at Harvey's place. I remember the scene like it was a photo I saw yesterday: two boxes of Propofol with all ten ampoules opened, emptied then carefully stowed back in the box; a syringe and drawing-up needle used to transfer the drug to the IV bag; a roll of strapping tape. That's it. All on the cabinet to the left of his bed and the IV bag set up just above it. All neat.'

'I know,' said Phil. 'I've seen the photos and I don't get it either.' Phil stopped there, looking down at his drink, closing his eyes, concentrating. Rob leaned over and placed a hand on Phil's shoulder. 'It's OK Phil, leave it for now.'

Phil looked at him. 'You said 'all neat'. What did you mean by that?'

Rob thought for a second. 'I don't know… just an impression I suppose. Everything was neat, orderly. No mess. Under control. Just what you'd expect of Harvey.'

'But how "under control" could Harvey have been?' Phil said, sarcastically. 'He'd had a skinful and gone home, made up a lethal cocktail, put a drip in his own left arm and let it run. No blood, no mess. Very considerate.'

Rob didn't say anything for a moment, just looked at Jess as she returned from the bathroom. 'Are you OK, Rob? You look like you're about to pass out,' she said.

'Sit down, Jess. I've got a really simple question for you – 'possible' or 'not possible' OK? Don't overthink it. Could you put a drip into your own dominant arm and hook up a bag of IV fluid without spilling blood as the IV went in?'

She gave Rob the strangest look. Part questioning, part revulsion, part disbelief, part knowing. 'Not possible.'

'And if you were drunk … beyond impossible,' he said.

Silence enveloped them where they stood at the end of a full bar. Harvey could not have been alone. The Ketamine trace was anything but innocuous. 'All neat' was really 'too neat'.

There was more to know.

Phil called the barman over.

'More drinks guys?' he asked.

'No, just a couple of questions,' said Phil.

Chapter 25

Questions

'OK, just give me a minute.' He moved off with a tray of glasses to be washed, pulled beers for a couple perched in the middle of the bar then headed out back to find someone to cover his break.

Rob had shifted in his seat. 'Phil, how much investigation was done on Harvey?'

'I'm assuming all the standard stuff was done,' Phil said. 'Obviously, I wasn't too close to this because I knew Harvey. I only assisted with some of the lab stuff and results. The crime scene, or at least death scene, and the examination, was all done by our assistant Coroner – and he's a veteran.'

'So, what does that mean in terms of investigation? Did he accept that Harvey's apparent suicide was just that or would he have considered it could've been staged?' asked Jess.

Phil picked up his phone and walked to the front window of the bar to make a call, looking out the window as he stood quietly talking. Jess and Rob remained silent.

After a while Phil gestured that he was going out to the car park and would return. He did so in a matter of minutes, carrying his laptop and took a seat at a table away from the bar. He called the others over.

His face said nothing special as he returned. 'The investigation was "uncomplicated" according to the investigating Coroner. I just rang him, and there was nothing at the scene to suggest anything other than a well-planned medical professional's suicide. He's sending me the full scene report by email now. We see a few of these every year, usually anaesthetists who kill themselves, and the scenes are typically clean and organised, no room for error, no mistakes with drug doses. No chance of survival. It's about as open and shut as our world gets.'

'Having said that,' Phil continued, 'we did all the usual stuff. Examine the body, temperatures, blood samples, the scene. In this case, the house got a good going over, and even the drug packaging was removed and dusted. Nothing turned up, guys.' He continued reading.

'There was nothing there to suggest that anyone else was involved in Harvey's death. If someone else had a hand in this, they were worryingly discreet.'

'But what about the Ketamine?' Rob was insistent.

'The only drugs that came back in Harvey's Tox screen were Propofol and Ketamine,' said Phil. 'And without the knowledge of the Ketamine, the investigator would not normally take a case like this any further. So, what are the possibilities? I know you said Harvey wouldn't touch K but you also would've said Harvey wouldn't kill himself. Either Harvey took the Ketamine himself or someone slipped it to him.'

Jess interjected. Clearly this was too much for her, too considered and too analytic. 'Harvey, for God's sake – he was smart, not stupid. Anyone with half a brain would not take Ketamine before trying to put a drip in themselves and start a lethal infusion. It's completely ridiculous! Harvey was murdered, for Christ's sake. The Ketamine was there because someone needed Harvey to cooperate. It's the most effective date-rape drug invented. Harvey scored a date with death.'

Rob and Phil looked at Jess, knowing she was correct.

It was Rob who broke the silence. 'So somewhere between drowning his sorrows here and getting home, Harvey was slipped something?'

Jess was furious. 'Well let's start with here'. 'Who was Harvey with?'

The bartender had started his break and now joined the trio, ready to answer their questions. 'My name's Steve.' He shook their hands.

'Steve, I'm Phil Vancleef and, although this is off the record, I need to let you know that I work for the State Coroner's office and Forensic Institute. A big part of what we do is to investigate suspicious deaths. There are a few details around Harvey's death that we need to clear up and hopefully you can help by telling us a bit more about that last afternoon he spent here.'

'Sure,' replied Steve. 'To be honest, there wasn't anything that remarkable about the afternoon. I see lots of guys in here searching for amnesia or something else at the bottom of a glass. Harvey was here for that. It was written all over him, and he was top-shelfing it. He had that beyond-angry look, you know, when someone is exhausted, but agitated. He was quiet. He watched the TV for a while sitting up here at the bar.'

'Was he talking with anyone,' asked Phil, 'anyone here or maybe on the phone?'

I remember he got a phone call and moved over to the couch. He was on the phone for a while and come to think of it seemed to have texts pinging off all afternoon. He had quite a few drinks, but I wouldn't say he was seven sheets till much later in the afternoon.'

'Was he with anyone?' Phil wanted to know.

'No, he was doing the solo-drunk thing. There weren't many in here that afternoon and most people who drink in the middle of the day stick to themselves. There was the guy who he left with later, though. They had a drink together and left soon after. I just assumed he was a pal that Harvey had organised to get him home.'

Rob looked around and saw the CCTV camera at the end of the bar. 'Phil, do you have jurisdiction to ask for the CCTV recordings here?'

'It doesn't much matter if you do,' responded Steve, before Phil had time to reply. 'That entire system is brand new – we were burgled last weekend and along with taking a huge pile of booze and cigarettes, the perps stuffed the alarm system and destroyed our monitoring gear. The new system went in on Monday.'

'Fuck it.' Rob was frustrated.

'How convenient.' Jess was livid.

Phil turned back to Steve. 'What can you tell me about the guy that Harvey met here, Steve?'

'Not much, really. Early fifties, white, average height and weight, suit with no tie. You know, average businessman-type.'

'Did he buy drinks?' asked Jess.

'Yeah, I think he bought a round of roadies for them,' replied Steve.

'How did he pay?' she continued. 'Did he use a credit card?'

'No chance,' laughed Steve. 'Lamaro's a tight Sicilian. The only way you get a credit card across the bar here is if you're running a tab for the night. A pair of roadies would have been cash on the bar.'

'So where do we go from here?' she asked Phil.

Phil thanked Steve. 'Can you write down your details and a contact number for me? I'll be in touch and we'll need to get back to you for a proper statement. OK?'

'No problem. Like I said, it's hard to believe.' He went back to work.

Rob had walked over to the front window to look up and down the street then returned to the bar, defeated.

'What is it?' Jess could probably guess.

'Not a CCTV camera in sight,' he replied.

Phil tapped the coaster on the bar. 'I've got another thought. Our mystery man who left with Harvey has to be involved and probably slipped him the ketamine here. Who would've known Harvey was here? Who would he have told?'

'His phone!' Jess held her mobile up to them. 'His phone is the answer. The only way anyone could've known Harvey was here was if he told them.'

'You're right,' said Rob. 'Harvey wasn't picking up calls that afternoon.'

Phil woke up his iPad and opened the email from his office that contained the scene report from Harvey's home. He opened the attached pdf and read through. He pawed through the report twice. 'No phone. There was no mobile phone retrieved in Harvey's belongings.'

'I don't believe this.' Rob needed another drink. 'There's too much stacking up here. These aren't coincidences.'

Phil was on the phone again. Ten minutes later, after talking to his office and the lead Coroner, he came back to Jess and Rob. 'I'll have a report on Harvey's phone activity inside an hour.'

Rob and Jess just looked at each other. Impressive.

Just over an hour later Phil's phone pinged as the email came through. He opened his iPad and the email with the attached pdf.

'You guys know I'm not showing you this,' he said cryptically. 'What you're about to see you just noticed 'cos I had my iPad open, right?'

'That's my recollection,' said Rob.

They scanned the page together.

3/5/19. 2pm to 6pm. There were eight missed calls from various numbers. Texts from an overseas number that they thought was French. Four voice mail messages. One incoming voice call from a local landline at 3.29pm and one outgoing at 3.35pm. Five outgoing text messages. Then nothing.

Jess looked over his shoulder. 'Rob, that's your number, 2.06pm.'

'Yeah, I sent him a message about catching up for a few sets.'

'Did he get back to you? Oh, he must have, there's an outgoing from him to you at 2.10pm.'

Rob nodded. 'I think he said he was up for it but that he was getting wasted at …' He didn't finish the sentence.

For the second time that day Jess's face was white with fear and anger and clarity. 'That number, the outgoing at 3.35pm. It's the executive suite at Queens.'

She opened her phone and searched the Queens website for the executive profile photos as she walked over to the bar.

'Steve, have you ever seen this guy?'

The barman identified Fenland without hesitation and she moved back to Rob and Phil.

'What's the next step for you?' she asked Phil.

'The investigating officer will get notified today,' he replied 'and given the Ketamine possibility and your theories about a staged suicide, I am sure they will interview Fenland asap. Where to from there will depend on what he's got to say.'

'Would you have thought of Fenland as a murderer?' Rob asked Jess.

'Not at all,' she said. 'I think he's more the crawling toady, gofer type – I don't see him having either enough to lose or the balls required to kill someone and, in this case, I certainly don't think he'd have had the technical wherewithal. But hey, you never know.'

Phil drained the rest of his beer. 'Guys I'm going to hit the road. I wasn't planning to go in to work today, but I need to get this moving up the line. Now. It's possible we're barking up the wrong tree completely, but I'd like to be sitting in the corner of Fenland's office tomorrow morning when the boys turn up for a chat without an appointment.'

'Me too, buddy.' Rob almost smiled. 'And we need to get some shopping done and get home – we've got friends coming for dinner. Keep us informed, eh?'

Outside the bar, Jess paused. 'Rob do you mind picking up the shopping and meeting me at home? I forgot to bring home a report I need to complete before tomorrow, and I need to duck into work to collect it. I won't be long.'

Chapter 26

Fenland

Fenland sat at his desk. By this time he was usually getting ready to go home, but the day had been all over the place. In fact, the whole of the last week, since Pearce's death, had been more than a little chaotic.

Just then Jess Goldman put her head through the open doorway, saw he was at his desk and walked in, closing the door behind her.

'I'm sorry Dr Goldman, but I am – '

'Don't bother, Fenland. She walked to the window and drew the shades. 'Sit back down – I think we have a couple of things to discuss. My meeting, my agenda. Understand?'

Fenland tried to wrangle back control of the situation. 'Look I know you're probably upset about Professor Pearce's death and – '

'You are more stupid than I thought possible, you piece of low-life shit.' Jess breathed in. Settled. She was going to take her time with this. 'Just sit down and listen or I walk back out the door and your life as a free man and that of your friends ceases to exist.'

Sweat was appearing on Fenland's face. The expression was fear and he clearly didn't know which direction this confrontation was heading.

Step one, thought Jess. Inject fear. Her skills were still there. 'So, let's start from the beginning, shall we?' She moved a chair from in front of his desk to beside it, close enough to be intimidating, far enough to be safe, odd enough to be unnerving.

He tried to turn his chair to face her, but Jess took one step and kicked it straight, nearly toppling Fenland out and causing him to grip both arms. He froze.

Step two, she thought. Rattle the cage.

'So right about now you're thinking, "What is this bitch on about and how much does she know?" Well, the answer is "enough to fuck up your life."' She had his undivided attention.

'Let's start with motivation. Harvey was a smart guy. You thought you could control him by bringing him up here and swamping him in a review that would take months. You knew you needed to keep a lid on the fuckups and corruption and crime in the health sector for long enough for things to work out for your friends on the hill and their connections. You didn't bet on Harvey's efficiency and persistence, and when the story broke publicly in the papers, someone assumed he was the source. He had to be silenced.'

Fenland's eyes widened. He became pale. Pitiful, thought Jess, this guy is scared, not mad. A dogsbody, not a doer. Weak, but locked into a game he's not strong enough to play.

'So, you met him at Lamaro's, slipped him the Ketamine and drove him home. What did you think would happen next, Fenland? Were you there? Did you stay for the staging? For the big event? Or did you leave that to others? Did you know what would happen? Did you care?'

'What do you want from me?' He had the poor sense to attempt a jeer.

Jess thought for a moment. 'Your problem, Fenland, is that you're not smart enough, just not professional enough. You're a rank amateur. And, what's more, I'm not the same as Harvey. I'm not the noble warrior Harvey was – in fact the last thing I really want is to spend my life in this business, suffering under pricks like you. I'm much more open to a well-financed, different kind of life. A pleasant, simple life somewhere with a nice climate, perhaps. Do you understand now what I want? What I want you and your connections to help with?' Jess paused and looked around, as though sizing up the office for the first time.

'You know, Fenland, I was talking this afternoon with an old buddy who just happens to work at Lamaro's. You were there that Friday afternoon, taking a drunk Harvey out the door, all nicely captured on CCTV, which also makes you the last person to have been seen with him. I am certain that's something the police would be interested in.'

'Bullshit,' blurted Fenland, 'the CCTV was … '

'What?' Jess rewarded him with a sardonic smile. It had almost been too easy. 'You half-wit fuck,' she said. 'There's only one way you could know about any problem with the CCTV. I think it's time to talk seriously, don't you?'

'You're off your fucking head.' He licked his lips furiously. 'You have no idea who or what you are dealing with. You can't threaten the type of people involved in this unless you want the same treatment as Pearce.' He reached for his mobile phone.

Jess knew she had enough. 'I don't think so,' she said, taking her mobile out of her jacket pocket. Two clicks and she stopped the recording and opened the send screen – a loaded weapon, holding it in his face.

Fenland sat back, terrified, defeated. His options were gone. 'OK, OK, I'm not the one you need to talk to – what do you want?'

'Nothing,' she said, and pressed send.

Jess looked at him with contempt.

'The way I see this working is that the police will be here to talk to you soon enough. You're not going to make any phone calls because, right now, you're going to think about your options. I'm betting you're a middle guy in this game. So, you're the one that's been identified, taking Harvey out of the bar. You'll be the one they question. Traffic cameras will track your car from Lamaro's to Harvey's house. Maybe the neighbours will have a security camera showing you entering his house. Don't think for a minute, Fenland, that the police won't track every connection you have and every call you made. You aren't smart enough to have covered your tracks that well. At the very least you'll go down as an accessory to murder.' Jess tilted her head in feigned concentration.

'So, what's the option? The smart one is to get yourself a lawyer and a deal. You'll bring the house down around the arseholes that are behind this miserable mess.'

Jess turned and walked out. She had friends coming for dinner.

Chapter 27

Cut the Crap - INTEGRITY

Elli contacted Charlotte in the middle of the following week and sent the final draft of Harvey's last podcast. It was Charlotte's idea to ask Alex Bonito to present the work, and Alex was happy to help. Publicity around Harvey's death caused a peak in downloads and subscriptions to his podcasts, and the editorial team at Loquitur developed an edited and abridged version of the talks, which they published on Harvey's home page.

―⋀⋁⋀―

I had never thought that one day I would present a podcast, and it is with a mixture of sadness and pride that I bring this work to you. My name is Dr Alex Bonito and I'm a friend and colleague of Harvey Pearce. Many of you will have heard the sad news of Harvey's recent passing. This tragedy represents a great loss to the many people who loved and were loved by Harvey, and a great loss to the patients and the health systems that Harvey worked so hard for. Many of us will miss him – his wisdom, his willingness to help and his wit. It is with pride that I had the opportunity to know Harvey well enough to deliver the last of this series of podcasts. He prepared this work in the final week of his life and it speaks to us of the core of his thinking. Harvey spent much of his work life involved in governance and quality and safety, and it is in this area that he pursued critical issues in the weeks and months prior to his death. His work translated directly into better and more reliable clinical outcomes for patients. Harvey's longstanding and germane philosophies, which he has made available through these podcasts, come together around the quality of integrity. This is the linchpin in his way of thinking about life and about how to live a simpler, better and more honest life. Not through commitment to a specific faith, or through fear of an uncomfortable after life ... No, Harvey's commitment came from a simple conviction that doing the right thing and removing the games and manipulations from life was what the world needed. Not a lot to ask, I thought, but quite often a challenge for us all to live up to. And yes, he lived this commitment in his work. But more than that, this was Harvey's approach to life. Now to Harvey's words ...

I have left the idea of integrity to last in this series of podcasts. If I had covered it first, it could be argued that there was nothing more to say, because it's true that this is without doubt the quality that matters most. It is simply the quality of being honest and having sound moral and ethical principles. The degree to which we apply integrity defines the goodness of our life. The simplicity of this definition has no regard for the great challenge that these qualities present to us in our modern world, where we see at every turn the normalisation of ruthless, driven behaviour that lacks ethical grounding. From political settings to our workplaces, schools and communities, on a daily basis we are confronted by behaviours that scream dishonesty, deception, corruption.

To most of us the idea of leading a moral life is not something we stop to consider regularly so it should not come as a huge surprise to find that when we find a crap-filled moment of life, there will have been a moral basis to that situation. Morality is not a complicated concept and it is not a sanctimonious construct that only works for those who are holier-than-thou. It doesn't relate to any god, necessarily, and is fundamentally agnostic. It's really just about right or wrong, good or bad.

You might wonder, what is right and what is wrong, what is good and what is bad? My version of right and good is different to yours. My tolerance of wrong or bad is not yours. We navigate this by starting with honesty applied inwardly, in our own deliberations.

If only it were that simple. The problem is that sitting right over the top of our personal honest evaluation of a moral question is a set of beliefs. Take, for example, the gun question. I might say that general access to guns in the community is wrong, because in my view there is no fundamental good in a gun. Guns hurt people – that is bad. Simple. Your answer to that may be that access to guns allows the community to protect itself from a disproportionate badness, with the balance of the argument falling towards overall community benefit.

So, your belief system, built upon life experience or maybe an inner principle or commitment sways your thinking towards an acceptance of guns. The challenge I propose here is to pare back, to lay aside the influence of a belief or faith system and look at the good or bad or right or wrong of the core question. Back at the gun … Can you say with honesty that a gun is for good?

This honesty is what lies at the heart of integrity. There is no acceptable reason for playing with the truth. The truth is what it is. It can't be altered or massaged or dealt with in fractions. Rumours, gossip, innuendo, half-truths, all undermine our integrity. The truth may be difficult to accept or difficult to deal with and it may be a more problematic reality for us at times. There are many occasions in life when bending or ignoring the truth creates what appears to be an easier path; however, it's inevitable that taking this direction will lead us to a wrong place eventually. We'll need to back track at some point and find the correct path.

Why are we attracted to untruths or bending the truth? We all do it from time to time. We embellish, we twist the facts, we lie, we add or subtract to make an impact or win an argument, to influence. If we stop for a moment and ask ourselves if this is the right thing to do, our inner self will give the right answer, so why do we even contemplate the lie in the first place?

Much of what I have talked about in these podcasts suggests that we need to spend more time in introspection, and I believe this is the answer to the question I have just posed. We've become distracted from our inner compass – the one that drives our ethical direction. As a result, our balance is disturbed, and the path we take is too fluid, too ready to be varied to suit ourselves and our goals or the pressures of our world.

I don't know if this is right, and I only have my thoughts and beliefs to work by, but here goes. If I was to ask the question 'What has changed about the way we consider morality?'

Does the answer lie in the movement of society away from classical religion over the last hundred years? Does it lie in less social interest in philosophical thought? Does it lie in the pace and competition of the modern world? Is it the natural way for humans to drift towards ruthless immorality?

Maybe the answer lies in a combination of all these things and more, and maybe the answer is less important than a strategy to help us reset. Although we may understand our present a little better through an appreciation of the mechanisms of social change, this can't change our present without an effective and present strategy and actions.

So, in the absence of us all having a common and agreed understanding of why integrity is a value that seems less important to the modern world, maybe the best we can do is say 'cut the crap'. Perhaps the simple solution to the moral 'drift', the parsimony with the truth, is to challenge ourselves and others to cut the crap and be honest.

More importantly we need to cut the crap of not caring about integrity, and to challenge our inner self regularly: Is my motivation correct? Am I being honest with myself? Am I bending the truth? Is my goal good or bad? Will I cause benefit or will I cause harm? How much do I value my own integrity?

These self-examinations don't always come easily (or at all for some of us) and, like many skills in life, need to be trained and practiced. It might come through meditation, mindfulness or just stopping now and then to ask ourselves a question. It doesn't matter. What's important is to be in touch with our own motivations and ethics and to look at our lives as if we were advising our best friend. The advice I would give to my best friend should be good enough for me!

The extension of this thought is to see ourselves in the place of another and to think about our speech and actions from their perspective and in consideration of the impact upon them. Empathy. Much of our modern world is characterised by disconnections rather than connections. Lack of empathy is entirely about lack of connection to others and to the impact of our actions on the world. We are not connected well enough to anticipate or appreciate the other perspectives. How often do we say something that causes hurt because we fail to think of the impact on another? To the other person this is a double injury from both the content of what is said and our failing to consider the impact of that content.

After all, this is similar to the 'little' deviations from truth, the lapses in integrity that don't seem to matter to us, but which may have significant impacts on others. Our connections to the world beyond us and our monitoring of our impacts is blunted by the gratification of our relatively small and isolated personal experience. We need to accept that this is a crap situation that deserves a remedy – a remedy that is not much more than cultivating awareness beyond ourselves, with that awareness being the beginning of consideration and compassion for the 'big world' as well as meeting the needs of our 'little world'.

It's easy for me to make sense of this at a personal level. It strikes me as a fairly intuitive and principled approach. Do good not bad, preserve the truth, consider the world, the big picture, others. But then I am struck by the complexity of the 'big world'. If I do this here then what will be the impact elsewhere? If I create an industry here that competes with an industry elsewhere, some workers will win, and some will lose. Some will have jobs, some will lose jobs. Some will prosper, some will be hurt. So how do I resolve a moral or ethical dilemma?

First, know that raising the moral dilemma as a question implies consideration of the big world. That's a good start, but it doesn't answer my question. Much has been written by many wise people about moral and ethical dilemmas, but because this is my podcast, I get to distil this in a way that I can understand.

I start by thinking about a change as having a driver based on improvement. Why would you change if not to improve?

Improvement means benefit, but not always for all, and comes at a cost, which is recouped in efficiency or value. Otherwise, again, why would you change something?

The benefit can be measured in net terms. The overall impact of the change is positive and sustainable despite some costs and or harm to some people. This is simply solving the utilitarian component of the dilemma.

The final part of the solution is to think about the proportional impact of the negative effects and their tolerability. By this I mean, does the whole community incur a proportionally fair and tolerable impact, taking into consideration the vulnerabilities of its parts? To answer this we need to call on our humanism and respect for others and also our ability to analyse empathically, because what we're aiming to avoid is disproportionate cost or an impact that's intolerable to some. We need to connect to others, to listen and hear.

In implementing an improvement, the costs (which may be monetary, quality of life, social, emotional) must be distributed without disproportionate or intolerable impact. In figurative terms we don't steal from the poor to make the rich richer, but taxing some from all (and a little more from the rich) to benefit everyone is a good approach!

Now, although truth, honesty and empathy are a huge component of integrity, and although I have proposed a two-minute approach to solving ethical dilemmas, these things are not the whole story.

All of our actions have consequences. A part of integrity is the accountability and responsibility for those consequences. Even with the best intentions, it is probable that things will not work out perfectly. That's OK, as long as we haven't been negligent and as long as we're prepared to accept responsibility to modify, fix, improve. This is accountability.

It's a vital part of our connection – we don't do something and walk away without a care. We monitor, watch, review, modify and nurture what we do so that we achieve the benefit we anticipate and at the same time avoid harm that may have an inherent risk associated with an action. We have the humility that is required to acknowledge when we're wrong and to allow us to seek help and correction. We care about the outcome, we have empathy for others and for the environment and context of our existence, and we have conscious consideration of the attainment of good.

How do we achieve this level of accountability – is it innate or do we learn it? How do we learn about integrity?

We have a starting point. As children we have some sense of ethics and morals – usually based on the palpability of an outcome – something hurts or helps, brings pleasure or pain and so on. As we get older others teach us about these things – parents, teachers at school. So, for most people there is a level of internal awareness and a receptivity to learning. There are a few people who are by nature, and to a lesser extent by nurture, unable to develop integrity and whose lives bring misery to those around them. There are many who allow integrity to be compromised by ambition, drive, pride, greed, bitterness or intolerance.

As we grow from childhood, we become more exposed to leaders in our world who teach us about integrity. In the everyday, where we work and live, there are leaders who teach good and bad lessons about integrity. In the broader world, political leaders and prominent individuals model integrity, or not.

Integrity is in large part learnt from these experiences through leaders who are true to the values of a community or organisation and live with honesty and commitment. They lead by example and through the quality and correctness of their speech and actions. These leadership strengths are more effective than the exercise of power and command. Leaders that model integrity believe what is right, say what they believe and do what they say. Their honesty is to be relied upon, as is their commitment to growth and benefit. They are builders with a robust moral and ethical foundation and who understand the strategies needed to solve ethical and moral dilemmas. They will choose the tougher pathway if that's needed to lead well. They don't buckle to politics, influence or contrived correctness. There won't be shortcuts. They have awareness, empathy and compassion, which they live and share.

We learn from people like this, who are uncommon in our world, and we become like them by conscious effort and work in our own lives. Stopping, thinking, deciding, changing.

If we do this, we will contribute to a culture of integrity.

We will reject communities or organisations that are incapable of integrity – organisations that flounder and never seem to move forward. Their culture resists change, crushes innovation and drives status quo. They support supporters of this culture and reject the rest. They do what is necessary to satisfy the masters but if you take a close look, they will lack ethical robustness, commitment, diligence, proactiveness, professionalism, respectfulness and diversity. They're not truly 'caring' places or people.

And the alternative? Yes, we will grow a culture of integrity characterised by honesty, commitment, diligence, reliability, valuing others, caring about what we achieve.

What makes some like this and others not? What makes this approach rub off on others, and what makes whole organisations or social groups places of integrity?

Perhaps empathy, perhaps compassion, perhaps leadership – I don't know for sure, but I do know that lack of integrity and lack of a positive culture is a palpable problem today. It's too easy for us to lose sight of the impact we have on others (and ourselves) and too easy to accept the failings and imperfections of our systems without confronting the truth and without a thought to solutions.

So, dear audience, I conclude here and thank you for your patience and interest and support. These words started as thoughts then became a talk at a conference and now somehow have become something more. I hope they help you. They have helped me to approach my life in a way that is more constructive. Because our world is so often more complicated than it needs to be, my goal has been to try to communicate what I hope is a simple and intuitive strategy. I don't know if I've been successful in that goal, but what started as my impatience and an intemperate need to just cut though crap seems to have come to a more considered place.

I have said we need to be prepared to challenge and confront what needs to change.

I have said that we need approach truth and knowledge with honesty.

I have said we need to value our world and each other and the resources we hold in trust for the future.

I have said that we need to be prepared to resolve the unnecessary complexity of the world, and, finally, I have said we need to frame these changes in a culture of integrity.

At each level we need to identify and cut the crap. All the stuff we allow to become the drivers of life, things we accept as the given way, but are often constructs driven by profit, a market, wrong thought or ill consideration. All the things we know at first blush are on the nose, too complex, contrived, misleading, wrong, unnecessary. We need to see them, call them for the crap they are, confront them and their merchants, and walk away from them. There is a nobler way, a more sustainable and happier way to live.

Approach any situation by simply considering five concepts: Truth, Challenge, Sufficiency, Simplicity, Integrity, and I suspect the answers you seek will appear.

This has been Harvey Pearce. I wish you happiness and a crap-free life.

Chapter 28

Sunday 8 December 2019

Jess and Rob pulled up seats at their usual table in the weak morning sun in the courtyard at Noshry. Summer was trying to arrive but had some way to go. Jess lay claim to a copy of the Sunday Sydney Morning Herald while Rob was door-stopped by an ex-colleague from the EMS.

'How long's it been now?' asked the paramedic whose name had embarrassingly slipped from Rob's mind.

'Oh, I've been out for just over five months. The opportunity was there and I was ready to move.' Rob wondered if this would end up yet another one of those 'well-done-you, you're-missed, brave-move, wish-I'd-done-it-myself' conversations.

'What are you doing with yourself?' asked nameless.

'I took a team management and combined clinical role in medic-star,' replied Rob. 'I really enjoy the critical-care space and it's a good organisation – good culture, understands teamwork, good mix of medical and nursing staff as well as paramedics and pilots, and no shortage of integrity and good systems. Pretty much ticked all the boxes the EMS missed!'

'Well good for you,' said Pat. That was his name.

'Have a good day, Pat. Oh, by the way let me know if you're looking for a change of employer!'

Rob moved to where Jess sat reading the newspaper and felt the familiar flatness that came with that conversation. It would take time. He was still grieving for a lost friend, shaking off the dust of his EMS career, adjusting to a new job, and trying to care a little less about the people who'd screwed up this town over the last year. From the look on Jess's face as she read the Sunday Supplement, he didn't hold out hope for a rapid change. 'What is it?' he asked

She didn't reply, absorbed in the content of the paper. She had ignored the front-page Armageddon piece on some new bat virus in China and flicked to page three. All he could see was the header: Government Fails on Governance

The article was written by Thomas Gallant. Rob remained none the wiser until Jess arrived at page three and came up for air.

'Rob, this is just incredible. Parts of this we know already, but, man, some of the connections in here are bizarre. Get me a coffee and some toast, will you honey?' she asked before she submerged again.

When he got back with their orders, Jess was about to erupt. 'OK, just listen.' She went back to the start of the article and began to trace her way through the paragraphs.

The new Government has announced a Royal Commission into ex-Premier Davidson over corruption links to the construction industry and unnamed underworld figures.

After Davidson and his government failed to be re-elected earlier this year in elections marred by serious allegations affecting the State's health system. Explosive details of corruption, health system failure and negligent indifference to patients' deaths and injuries were published by the SMH on 3 May 2019 and turned the tide against the Davidson government.

Soon after the release of this information, the well-known and highly respected Emergency Physician, Professor Harvey Pearce was killed. Dr Pearce was an outspoken advocate for excellence in patient safety and quality systems and, at the time of his death, was working on a comprehensive investigation into these matters. It is believed that Professor Pearce may have uncovered detail of the corrupt systems and connections behind this outrage and that parts of his findings informed the SMH exposé.

Professor Pearce was murdered and his death was staged to appear a suicide. But for keen forensic analysis and investigation by the Coroner's office, this crime may have gone undetected. The perpetrators are yet to be brought to justice, however, it is understood that because of the unusual methods employed in the crime, underworld medical or clinical connections are being explored.

Todd Fenland, a mid-level executive from Queens Hospital remains in custody awaiting trial for aiding and abetting the murder, but it is believed that he has struck a deal with the Office of The Director of Public Prosecutions. It is reported that after receipt of a clandestine recorded conversation and tip-off, subsequent evidence obtained from phone records and statements from witnesses in a city bar implicated Fenland in the murder of Professor Pearce.

Ex Health Minister Henderson and Mr Roger Hutten, the ex-CEO of Queens Hospital will give evidence in the first week of the commission's hearings.

Both Henderson and Hutten have been held in protective custody since June when they were arrested in connection with the death of Professor Pearce. They have been charged with conspiracy to murder and it is believed that further charges will be laid as a result of this investigation.

Hutten, Henderson and her venture-capitalist husband Peter Morricone, were reported to have been in a bizarre three-way sexual relationship and to have constructed a plan of self-promotion and a complex financial web involving funds from the construction industry and kick-back contracts. Significant offshore bank accounts have been frozen. Henderson's husband, whose finance domain has ties to the construction industry, has not been seen since late June. It has been revealed that Mr Morricone had connections with elements of the industry believed to be linked to underworld activity, including extortion, kidnap and murder.

There is also new evidence surrounding the renegotiation of incongruously favourable pay and conditions achieved by the construction workers union with the last government. Their plans to further influence the 2019 election were disrupted by publication of material in May by this journalist, which not only blew the whistle on health system's failures due to under-resourcing but also publicised simultaneous provision of generous and redundant construction contracts. Henderson was expected to have become Business and Planning Minister in the new government.

It is believed that Hutten's ex-wife Jane Chantier will provide evidence at the trial of her acrimoniously divorced husband and his high-flying lover. Ms Chantier was dismissed from her role as Health Secretary in July by the incoming government.

Her replacement is yet to be appointed; however, the Acting Health Secretary was interviewed last week and has indicated that a separate investigation and Royal Commission will be announced into a range of issues in the health system. These include systematic failure of executive and health department leaders' performance in ensuring patient safety. A radical overhaul of the EMS is also forecast in a statement from the Secretary 'to expose and eliminate drug abuse and to correct a culture of nepotism and secrecy. We will reinvigorate the EMS with a focus on quality and safety of patient care, whilst it deals with inherent cultural and professional challenges'.

Early reaction from the Health sector indicates cautious optimism among staff and management that this may be the first effective step towards long-lasting, effective reform.

The Acting Secretary concluded her statement by promising 'a new system that will permanently deliver reliable, high-standard care, which our community deserves, and which resources and supports our committed workforce effectively.'

Rob looked up from the coffee he hadn't touched. 'You know how proud I am of what you did in outing Fenland, Jess. It was smart and brave. Your talents are wasted, you know.'

'It wasn't rocket science,' she replied with a smile, 'but it did make me feel good.'

They finished their breakfast with not much more to say.

The sun was persisting but was confused by a light unseasonal sprinkling of rain. Everything about this year had been strange.

'Rob, you know what I think? Harvey's goal was unquestionable and was focussed on fixing things he saw that were wrong; building something that would last and making things better, period. If bad people got in the way of that, they wouldn't have been his target, but he also wouldn't have been sad that they were brought down in the process. He stuck to his guns and did what he had to … So, who was Gallant's source? Was it Harvey?' Jess said.

'Who knows? And does it really matter? I doubt that'll ever come out because it doesn't need to, and journalists don't talk. The courts will deal with this with the help of a few dirtbags who want to keep their sentences to a minimum.' Rob shifted in his seat and sipped his coffee. 'Maybe it wasn't one person. Maybe it was a combination of bits of information from a stack of leads and leaks. It isn't that complicated, really. People love to talk, and to listen. Either way, it seems the truth has a way of emerging.'

www.ingramcontent.com/pod-product-compliance
Lightning Source LLC
LaVergne TN
LVHW040137080526
838202LV00042B/2942